W9-BZF-087

"A vicious concoction of half-truths and fictitious garbage was written by you and printed in a national newspaper for the world to see."

Emma winced. It was true. She couldn't deny it.

"You are lucky I didn't personally sue you for slander."

But she didn't feel lucky. Not at all. At the time, losing her job had felt like the biggest calamity that could ever befall her. Now she knew it was just the start of her troubles.

A couple of seconds passed. Leo picked up a pen and tapped it on the desk.

"If that is all you came to say, I believe our business is concluded."

"No." Emma's stomach tightened. If only it were that straightforward. "That is not all I came to say. There is another matter we need to discuss."

"Go on."

The weight of his gaze felt heavy enough to flatten her, every nerve-filled second dragging longer than the last. She took a brave breath.

"I am pregnant." The words felt like boulders in her mouth, too big, too unruly. "I am going to have a baby."

Andie Brock started inventing imaginary friends around the age of four and is still doing that today—only now the sparkly fairies have made way for spirited heroines and sexy heroes. Thankfully, she now has some real friends, as well as a husband and three children, plus a grumpy but lovable cat. Andie lives in Bristol and when not actually writing might well be plotting her next passionate romance story.

Visit the Author Profile page
at Harlequin.com for more titles.

Andie Brock

FROM EXPOSÉ TO EXPECTING

If you purchased this book without a cover you should be aware
that this book is stolen property. It was reported as "unsold and
destroyed" to the publisher, and neither the author nor the
publisher has received any payment for this "stripped book."

HARLEQUIN®
PRESENTS®

Recycling programs
for this product may
not exist in your area.

ISBN-13: 978-1-335-40370-4

From Exposé to Expecting

Copyright © 2021 by Andrea Brock

All rights reserved. No part of this book may be used or reproduced in
any manner whatsoever without written permission except in the case of
brief quotations embodied in critical articles and reviews.

This is a work of fiction. Names, characters, places and incidents
are either the product of the author's imagination or are used fictitiously.
Any resemblance to actual persons, living or dead, businesses,
companies, events or locales is entirely coincidental.

This edition published by arrangement with Harlequin Books S.A.

For questions and comments about the quality of this book,
please contact us at CustomerService@Harlequin.com.

Harlequin Enterprises ULC
22 Adelaide St. West, 40th Floor
Toronto, Ontario M5H 4E3, Canada
www.Harlequin.com

Printed in U.S.A.

FROM EXPOSÉ TO EXPECTING

For anyone who has bought my books, read my books or supported my writing career in any way. It is much appreciated.

CHAPTER ONE

THE ENORMOUS BUNCH of flowers wobbled through the air. Without thinking, Emma stepped forward, her arms outstretched, ready to catch it. Her fingers managed to grab hold of the twisted stems, but the weight took her by surprise and she had to clasp the bouquet to her chest to stop it from toppling forward. Only then did she wonder what on earth she thought she was doing.

For a moment she stood there, feeling silly, the crushed blooms held tightly, hopefully, like she was expecting some sort of reward. A future husband possibly. Ha!

But no one was looking at her. All eyes had turned to the woman who had thrown them. On the other side of the security barriers a beautiful female with tumbling dark hair was having a full-on argument with the security guards.

'Do you have any idea who I am?' Her

voice echoed around the atrium. 'My name is Vogue Monroe and I've a good mind to have you both sacked.' She positively shimmered with rage, glaring at the guards with flashing eyes and a heaving chest.

Vogue Monroe. Emma had guessed right. Hollywood actress and latest in a long line of stunning women to be romantically linked with Leonardo Ravenino. She edged closer for a better look.

'I'm sorry, miss, it doesn't matter who you are, you are not coming in without an appointment.'

'Fine. Whatever.' Vogue held up her hands, nails like talons. 'But you can give him a message from me.' She tossed her head, dark curls rippling down her back. 'You can tell Leonardo Ravenino that he is nothing but a…a selfish, arrogant, egotistical bastard.' She paused for dramatic effect. 'You can tell him that I actually feel sorry for him. Because he is emotionally sterile, incapable of forming a real relationship with anyone because the only person he loves is himself!'

It was an award-winning performance—Emma had to give her that. And she had certainly got everyone's attention, as a quick glance at the row of receptionists along one wall revealed. They retained a professional air, but their hands on their keyboards had stilled.

'And you can tell him…' Her piercing gaze now fell on Emma, her green eyes flicking from the bouquet still held in Emma's arms to Emma's startled face. 'You can tell him *exactly* what he can do with his flowers.'

Well! Emma stood rooted to the spot. If only she worked for one of the tabloids this would be pure gold.

But Emma Quinn didn't work for the tabloids. She was junior features reporter for the *Paladin* newspaper. A serious, well-respected publication with a politically and socially well-informed readership. She was here to do an interview with Leonard Ravenino on renewable energy. Except he was already over two hours late. If Ms Monroe did but know it, even if she had managed to gain entry to Raven Enterprises, her ex-lover was not around to feel the weight of her wrath.

She watched as, with a final flourish, the actress exited the building, long legs folding themselves into a chauffeur-driven car waiting outside, tinted windows hiding her from view as the car pulled into the traffic.

Drama over, Emma turned back. Two hours of waiting meant she was familiar with every inch of Raven Enterprises' gleaming reception area. A sleek white desk ran along one side, where four receptionists, all dressed in black, quietly turned back to their work. One of whom, Nathalie, had been kindly trying to update Emma on Signor Ravenino's likely time of arrival. Even if she hadn't known herself.

But Emma would wait as long as it took. She was not going to let this opportunity slip through her fingers. Securing an interview with Leonardo Ravenino was the biggest coup of her journalistic career so far. The enigmatic Italian businessman gave very few interviews—in fact, he had a reputation for mistrusting the press. Emma had had the feeling, when her editor had set her the task, that he hadn't really thought she stood a cat in hell's chance—a bit like sending the new kid out for a tin of striped paint. But somehow, against the odds, she had done it. And she was *not* going to mess this up.

She had done her research, reading everything she could about this handsome billionaire. Far more than the interview called for, in fact. But she had found herself fascinated by the man. Fabulously wealthy but notoriously private, he had a penchant for dating high-profile women but loathed the tabloid press.

Even so, there was no shortage of pictures

of him, a different actress or socialite on his arm every time, a minor royal draped around his six-foot-four frame as they left a nightclub, or a fashion model lounging on the deck of his yacht, all tiny bikini and golden tan, caught by the powerful zoom lenses of the paparazzi.

Enigmatic was a word the tabloids bandied about a lot, so were *inscrutable*, *mysterious*. Charming when he chose to be but taciturn in equal measure. Rude even, especially when confronted with a microphone or a sea of camera flashes.

His background was puzzling too. It hadn't taken long for Emma to discover that he had been next in line to inherit the title of Conte di Ravenino, head of the Italian principality whose name he bore, which had been in his family since the sixteenth century. But for some reason he had turned his back on the place and walked away, the title going to his younger brother. Try as she might, Emma couldn't find out why.

'Would you like me to take that from you?' Indicating the heavy bouquet in her arms, Nathalie beckoned Emma forward. The two women exchanged a glance.

'All part of the job?' Emma raised her

brows enquiringly. 'Spurned lovers turning up, chucking flowers around?'

Nathalie laughed. 'Well, let's just say there's never a dull moment when Signor Ravenino is in town.'

'He has quite a reputation, I gather?' Emma perched herself on the edge of the desk.

'He is a force to be reckoned with, that's true,' Nathalie agreed. 'You'll see what I mean when you meet him.'

'If I ever get to meet him.' She pulled a face.

'I'm really sorry you have had to wait so long.'

'It's not your fault.' Emma hesitated. Maybe she could make use of all this hanging around by gleaning some more information about her subject. Purely in the interests of background research, of course. 'So, do you have to do a lot of this, apologising to people Signor Ravenino has kept waiting, making excuses, re-arranging schedules?'

Nathalie considered. 'He doesn't spend a lot of time in the UK office. But when he is here it's fair to say we earn our money.'

'He is a good employer?'

'Yes. As long as you don't mind working long hours. And having a positive attitude to some of his more challenging requests. You learn to expect the unexpected with Signor Ravenino.'

'What sort of challenges?'

'Oh, you know, arranging a private viewing at the Natural History Museum at a moment's notice. Flying a top chef to serve dinner on a remote Scottish island. He once bought every painting in an exhibition then wanted them hung in twelve different locations. That meant four different countries, two different continents! One of them is over there.' She pointed to a huge abstract canvas dominating the far wall.

'So, what Leonardo wants, Leonardo gets?'

'Something like that. But Mia, that's his PA here in the UK, is the one who has to deal with the more personal issues. The fallout from his complicated love life.'

'Would you say that Leonardo Ravenino treats women badly?'

'Not exactly.' Nathalie frowned. 'It's more that no woman ever manages to get him to behave the way they want him to behave. They all think they will be the one to tame him, to get him down the aisle, but they end up disappointed, just like all the others.' She glanced at the forsaken flowers on the chair beside her. 'Mia has the florist on speed dial.'

Emma followed her gaze. Clearly an exotic bouquet had done nothing to pacify the recipient in this instance. But this was all interesting stuff. She wanted to hear more. 'I'm guessing you must pick up a lot of stories working here.'

'Oh, yes.' Nathalie hesitated, suddenly wary. 'Though you're a reporter, aren't you? I probably shouldn't be sharing them with you.'

'Off the record. I promise.' Emma gave an encouraging smile. 'The piece I'm writing is about ocean thermal energy. Very dry. Well, very wet, but you know what I mean.'

Nathalie laughed. 'Okay.' She gave a quick glance to her side, lowering her voice. 'But you didn't hear this from me.'

Emma mimed her lips being zipped.

'Well…' Nathalie leaned forward conspiratorially. 'There was this one time…'

It was another hour before Leonardo Ravenino finally appeared. Emma had almost given up when a sleek black limo pulled up outside and in a flurry of movement a group of people entered. Moving forward like a swarm, Emma could just make out Leonardo in the centre, tall and dark, his shoulders back, his head held high, issuing orders to his minions as he marched through the echoing space.

She leapt to her feet, joining the edge of the throng, hurrying along beside them, her futile attempt at waving her notebook in the air going unnoticed. They were heading towards the elevator. If she wasn't careful, he was going to have disappeared before she had even had the chance to call out his name. The elevator doors opened and moving as one mass the group entered. No! Something told Emma that this was her one and only chance. If she let him get away now, she might as well kiss her interview goodbye.

The doors were almost closed when she stuck out her leg, jamming her foot between them. Immediately they opened again to reveal the group collectively staring at her, suddenly silent.

'Hi.' Emma gave a nervous cough. 'My name is Emma Quinn, from the *Paladin* newspaper.'

'Remove your foot from the elevator, young lady.' A heavily muscled man stepped forward, blocking her view.

'Yes, yes, of course.' Emma faltered. 'But I have an appointment with Signor Ravenino.' She fumbled in her jacket for her phone. 'Here, look.' She brought the screen to life with a shaking hand. 'This is the email confirmation. I've been waiting for ages.'

'Remove your foot from the elevator.' The guy didn't look remotely interested in her message.

'Yes, but—'

'I'll deal with this, Harry.'

The deep velvet tone, the faint Italian accent, there was no mistaking whose voice it was. Suddenly Leonardo Ravenino was standing before her, all sleek tailored suit, white shirt, perfectly knotted tie. Close up he was every bit as handsome as Emma had been led to believe, but it wasn't his beauty that took her by surprise, more the overpowering sense of *him*.

Nostrils slightly flared, thick, dark brows pulled together over narrowing eyes, his mouth tightly closed, there was an invincibility about him, as if nothing could touch him. Only his shadowed jawline gave any sign that it had been a long day, the close-cut stubble giving him a slightly feral, dangerous edge.

His gaze held hers steadily, dark and all-seeing. He gave a dismissive flick of his hand to the silent group still waiting in the elevator behind him, indicating they should go on without him.

'Ms Quinn, did you say?' His frown deepened as if he was trying to place her. Now that his full attention was trained on her he was even more formidable.

'Yes.' Emma swallowed. 'From the *Paladin*. We had an appointment for an interview.'

His puzzled expression was not encouraging.

'To discuss Raven Enterprises' investment in renewable energy?' Emma tried again. 'It was supposed to be at three o'clock.'

'Then please accept my apologies.'

'That's okay.' It wasn't actually. He had clearly forgotten all about her. Weren't people like him supposed to have a team of secretaries and PAs reminding him of his appointments? Why hadn't that Mia done her job? But he was here now, that was all that mattered. 'Perhaps we can do the interview now?'

'*Mi dispiace*… I am sorry, you misunderstand me. The interview will no longer be possible.' His lips set firmly.

'No!' In a rush of panic Emma grabbed hold of his arm, a gesture that was met with a small, pointed glance. She quickly removed it. 'I mean, it was all agreed.'

'Well, now it's unagreed.' For a moment it looked as though he was going to brush at his sleeve where her hand had been, but he resisted the temptation. 'I do hope you haven't been too inconvenienced.'

'No! I mean, yes, I have! We have to do this interview. You promised.' It wasn't the most grown up of replies, but panic was setting in fast.

'Time has unfortunately made it impossible.'

No, you are the one who has made it impossible. Emma swallowed down her rising anger. *And what's more, you don't even care.* He might be saying the right words, but his eyes held no hint of apology—more a sort of distracted indifference.

She bit down hard on her lip to stop herself from saying what she really thought. There was nothing to be gained by doing that.

'It needn't take long,' she implored. 'An hour, less even.'

'I'm sorry…'

'Well, later this evening perhaps.'

'If you will excuse me…'

'No!' As he started to move away, Emma reached out to grab his arm again, not caring any more what he thought.

'Signor Ravenino.' She tried to steady herself. 'I appreciate how busy you are, but the fact is I was promised an interview with you, I have been waiting for over three hours, and quite frankly I think it is incumbent on you to honour that arrangement.'

She released his arm, tucking her hair behind her ears, waiting.

At least she had got his attention back. She watched, barely breathing, as his leisurely gaze took her in. Slowly he crossed his arms over his chest, all studied nonchalance. Finally, a hint of a smile curved the corner of his finely drawn lips, like a cat playing with a mouse. 'Do you now?'

'Yes, yes, I do.' Emma felt a flush creeping up her neck. 'I think you owe it to me to give me at least an hour of your valuable time.'

He pushed back a starched white cuff to check the flashy timepiece on his wrist. Maybe there was a glimmer of hope.

'I can fit in with whatever you suggest.' Emma rushed to blow on the embers. 'I'm prepared to be flexible.'

One dark eyebrow rose. Emma felt her flush creep higher, but she stood her ground, refusing to acknowledge the way his tone had changed from one of irritation to something more like mild flirtation. Her stomach, however, was doing traitorous little leaps of interest.

'Very well.' He paused, giving her that look again. Assessing, stern but seriously hot. 'My nightclub, this evening.'

His nightclub? Taken by surprise, Emma tried to collect herself.

'To do the interview?'

'*Sì*, to do the interview.' He angled his head slightly, like he was dealing with someone who was a bit slow. Or, worse, someone who had jumped to the wrong conclusion. An awful thought that made Emma cringe. She countered it by putting on her most business-like voice.

'That would be acceptable.'

'*Bene.*' Leo made a small adjustment to his stance. He had a way of owning every movement, as if it was his alone.

'Shall we say eleven p.m.?'

Eleven o'clock? She was normally tucked up in bed long before that, reading a good biography or maybe a historical novel. Certainly not prancing about in nightclubs.

'Isn't that a little late?'

Leonardo's response was a take-it-or-leave-it shrug.

'Fine. Eleven o'clock. Thank you.' Why was she thanking him? *He* was the one who had let *her* down. Because he held all the cards, that's why.

'*Bene.*' Leonardo repeated the word. 'You know my nightclub?'

'Yes.' Emma nodded. Of course she did.

Hobo was one of the most famous clubs in London, much loved by the glitterati. Rumour had it that Leonardo had won it in a bet, though whether that was true or not Emma had no idea. Like so much about this man, it was shrouded in mystery.

'Then I will see you there. Don't be late.'

Her be late! The cheek of it! With his back turned he left Emma searching for a suitably tart retort, though nothing too contentious, of course. But the glance over his shoulder stole her thoughts. And her breath. His eyes twinkled with mischief. Devilment. He was teasing her. And it felt as if the ground had just shifted beneath her feet.

CHAPTER TWO

EMMA GLANCED AROUND HER. She felt completely out of place in this exclusive nightclub, even though she had been personally escorted to an empty upper seating area, well away from the dance floor and the thump of the bass that held the gyrating bodies in its thrall.

This area was all about comfort, padded red leather seating arranged around low tables, subdued lighting and carefully chosen artwork. More paintings from the exhibition Nathalie had mentioned, perhaps? A handsome waiter had taken her drinks order, the sparkling water arriving on a silver salver and placed before her with a theatrical flourish more suited to the finest champagne.

Emma took another sip. It was foolish of her to have arrived so early but the burning desire to get this interview in the bag had seen her head across town a good hour before she'd needed to. Faced with two liveried doormen, she had anticipated having to explain who she was, but one mention of her name had seen her politely ushered inside.

She stood up, moving to stand by the railing that overlooked the dance floor below. She had a good view from up here, but the dim lighting made it impossible to pick out any faces. Just a writhing sea of bodies, arms raised in the air, heads swaying, long hair tossed about. It looked fun, Emma had to admit. But not the sort of fun she would ever be part of.

Clubbing was not something she had ever done. Her life since she'd been in London had been all about getting some sort of education, finding a job and earning a living. There had been no time for frivolities such as this, even if she'd been able to afford them. Which she couldn't. In fact, this was the first time she had even so much as set foot in a nightclub. Not that she would be telling Leonardo Ravenino that.

'*Buonasera.*' The rich velvet voice came from right behind her, spinning Emma around. Standing very close, Leonardo leaned forward to greet her, kissing both cheeks, the Italian way. 'I hope I haven't kept you waiting?'

'No, not at all.' Not this time, anyway.

Emma collected herself. 'I've been watching the people on the dance floor.'

'Ah, yes.' He came and stood beside her, strong hands curling around the railing. 'Quite mesmerising, isn't it?'

Emma sneaked a look at his profile. All fluid grace and hard masculine lines beneath expensive Italian tailoring, it wasn't difficult to see why women fell at his feet. There was a dark, edgy energy about him, an inherent sexiness, that was very hard to ignore.

'Is it true that you won this nightclub in a bet?' She hadn't meant to plunge right in, or even ask this question at all, but somehow it had slipped out without warning.

Her companion turned his head, a hint of warning in the dark grey eyes. Had she overstepped the mark already? There was a moment's pause before he spoke again.

'I see the interview has started already, Ms Quinn.'

Emma silently rebuked herself. She should have been more subtle. But something about this man was jumbling her carefully planned questions. 'I just noted that it's a divergence from your other businesses.' She hurried to try and make amends. 'And wondered if hospitality was something you intend to invest more in in the future?'

An infinitesimal raising of one eyebrow told her he knew she was bluffing.

'No, I have no plans to go into hospitality. And for your information, Hobo was payment for a debt. Nothing more. You shouldn't believe everything you read in the tabloids.' His stare was one of rebuke. 'You of all people should know that.'

'Yes, of course.' Emma adjusted the cuffs of her jacket in a serious newspaper reporter kind of way.

'Shall we sit down?'

She let out a relieved breath, only to have it stolen again when Leonardo slipped a guiding arm around her waist to move her back towards the seats. A bottle of champagne had mysteriously appeared on a low table. Filling two glasses, Leo held one out to Emma, waiting as she sat down.

'Oh, no, thanks. I think I'll just stick to water.'

'That's very professional of you.' Leo seated himself opposite her. 'If a little disappointing.'

'Disappointing?'

'*Sì*. You see, I was hoping you would join me in a small celebration.'

'What are we celebrating?'

'A successful day.' He smiled, his lips

tightly closed, accompanied by a self-deprecating shrug that didn't fool Emma for one moment. She suspected that all his days were successful. That he made quite sure of it. Nevertheless, she accepted the glass and took a sip. It was delicious. Cold bubbles slid down her throat like silk.

Trying hard to ignore his long stare, she reached for her bag to pull out her trusty notepad and pen, and then, after a moment's hesitation, her cellphone.

'Is it okay if I record our conversation?'

'I don't see why not.' Leo crossed his legs, leaning back against the seat. Outwardly he seemed relaxed, but Emma had to be on her guard. She must not mess this up. Setting her phone on the table between them, she pressed record.

'So, Raven Enterprises invests in a number of different renewable energy companies. Would you say that was something you were particularly interested in?'

'The future of our planet is something we should all be interested in.' The reply came back slick and fast.

'Indeed.' Emma began to scribble down notes. A recording was great, but she liked to have everything down on paper too. Belt and braces. 'Raven Enterprises is something of a pioneer in the way it invests in start-up companies, rather than more established enterprises. Why is that?'

'I like to be in on something at the start. It's easier to control that way.' His tone was pleasant, easy. But control was clearly something this guy was all about. It was written in his every feature, every movement.

'And which sources of renewable energy do you think have the most potential for the future?'

'Biological proteins are interesting.' He paused and Emma felt the weight of his stare on her bent head. 'Tell me, Ms Quinn, do you always dress so conservatively?'

Her head shot up; her eyes trapped by his.

It was true that her outfit, navy skirt and fitted jacket, cream blouse, navy court shoes, did look rather out of place here. Briefly she had wondered if she should have chosen some sort of evening wear in view of the location and the time of day. But the fact was she didn't have any, or even enough time for a quick trawl of the local charity shop in search of a lucky find.

'This is my work outfit, Signor Ravenino. And, please, call me Emma.'

'Then you must call me Leo. So, do you never mix business with pleasure, Emma?'

Emma frowned. 'I take pleasure in my work if that's what you mean.'

This was certainly true. Working for the *Paladin* was not so much a pleasure as the realisation of her goal. And vindication, too, that all those awful jobs, living in dank little rooms, eating nothing but beans on toast, studying late into the night until her eyes hurt and her head throbbed had all been worth it. Because each of those things had taken her another step away from the chaos of her family background towards a shiny new future that was just within her grasp.

'Not exactly what I meant, no.' Leo leaned forward to top up her glass again. Emma was surprised to see it was almost empty. 'I just wondered if beneath that stern exterior there is a party girl waiting to get out.'

'No, there isn't.' She returned to her notepad. 'Could you elaborate on the role of biological proteins?'

'Do you like to dance, Emma?'

'No!' She straightened her notepad. This interview was not going the way it was meant to. 'I… I don't know how to dance.'

'Sure you do.' The gaze he aimed at her was like a full-on assault. Bold, roving, cocksure. Which no doubt he was. 'Everybody does. You just relax and let the music move you.' Suddenly on his feet, his hand stretched out towards her.

Emma stared at it in horror. Surely he wasn't expecting her to dance here, now? But the impatient little shake of his hand suggested he was.

'I don't think—' But even as she said the words she found herself rising, taking the outstretched hand, feeling it closing around hers.

The music was little more than a dull thud from up here, a pounding, incessant throb, like a heartbeat. Her own heart sounded almost as loud to her as Leo moved her closer, one hand resting on her shoulder, the other lightly pressed into the small of her back. It was a respectful hold, guiding rather than intimate, but that didn't stop Emma's panic. He was so close she could hear his every breath, feel the heat from his body. And he smelled divine. Relaxed muscles moved effortlessly, taking her with him, small movements drawing her closer still until she had no choice but to tentatively snake her arms around his waist to sway with him.

'Now, where were we?'

He was speaking over the top of her head, and it took Emma's addled brain a moment to work out that he was talking about continuing the interview. This was crazy, he was crazy.

Expect the unexpected, wasn't that what Nathalie had said? And one thing was for sure, she had never expected to conduct the interview like this. If anything, she had worried he might be rather closed, hard to talk to. Instead he was all relaxed charm, answering politely, though admittedly giving little away. She took a moment to breathe. At least focussing on her questions would take her mind off her rioting senses.

Pulling back a little, she prepared herself to address the wall of his chest. 'Does Raven Enterprises intend to extend its investment to other potential energy sources?' Somehow she managed to drag the question up from somewhere.

'I'm always open to new ideas.' His body rocked gently to one side. 'You have to look at the scientific evidence and decide which one to back. A bit like horse racing.'

'Would you say you were a gambling man?'

'There is a certain thrill in taking a chance.' She could hear the confidence in his voice. 'And satisfaction when it pays off.'

'And when it doesn't?'

'Then you move on, Ms Quinn. Life is too short to agonise over failures.' His hand fell from her shoulder. 'More champagne?'

'No!' She moderated her voice. 'No, thank you. But I would like to sit down now.'

'Of course.' Leo gave a small accepting shrug.

Suddenly the air seemed terribly hot. Taking off her jacket, Emma laid it neatly on the seat beside her, undoing the top button of her blouse. That was better. Marginally. She reached for her notepad again, determined to ignore the way Leonardo was watching her every move. She crossed her legs, cleared her throat, pen ready.

Leo surveyed the *Paladin*'s junior reporter through lowered lashes. She was an interesting subject. Despite losing the jacket, she managed to look more prim than ever, her defences pulled firmly around her. If his suggestion of a dance had been to make her feel less ill at ease, it had clearly failed. But despite her conservative clothes and haughty manner there was something inherently sexy about her—the pout of her lips, her habit of nipping the bottom one with small white teeth when she was thinking. The way she looked up at him through that fringe…

She had a refreshing lack of conceit, as if she paid no heed to her natural beauty. And she was bright too. Leo ran his hand across his chin. No, the dance hadn't been about settling her nerves. It had been about him. He just couldn't help himself.

Today had been manic but successful. His favourite sort of day. Deliberately packing everything into the shortest possible time frame was the way he liked to work. He thrived on the pressure and seeing how other people coped with it. It sorted out the weak from the strong. And sometimes, like today, working at speed meant closing a deal before a rival company got a look in. Which was always satisfying.

He'd forgotten all about this interview. If his secretary hadn't been so busy no doubt she would have cancelled it. If Ms Quinn hadn't been so persuasive when he had come upon her in the foyer of Raven Enterprises, he would have dismissed her. He had only agreed to do it in the first place to try and silence a few board members who were starting to make noises about the lack of positive publicity. Too many photos of him coming out of nightclubs were not good for the confidence of investors, apparently.

Tempted though he was to tell them his private life was none of their business, Leo knew that where money and leadership was concerned, no one, no matter how powerful, was totally immune. So when an email from the *Paladin* happened to arrive straight after another tedious board meeting, he had agreed to the interview. An article about Raven Enterprises' investment in renewable energies. What could be more positive than that?

And Ms Emma Quinn was certainly very thorough. The questions had been coming at him hard and fast for some time now.

'Clearly you are interested in the future of our planet and yet you own a private jet, you fly all over the world. Does that not bother your conscience?'

She briskly flipped over the page of her notebook, tucked her hair behind one ear, her pen held in position. Like he wasn't going to notice the barb held in her question.

'You are assuming I have a conscience, Ms Quinn.'

The pen stopped scratching across the paper, but she didn't look up. Instead a stillness came over her, as if she was holding herself in check.

Leo did the same. He should fight the desire to play cat and mouse.

'International travel is a necessary evil in the world of business,' he continued. 'A private jet saves time, it's as simple as that.'

'And the flashy cars, the luxury yacht?' Now she came back at him, going for the

jugular this time. He couldn't resist a coun-
terattack.

'It's true, fast cars are a weakness of mine.'
He gave her a small but deadly smile. 'I never
said I was perfect.'

He watched with satisfaction as those full
lips pursed, the effort of not saying what she
wanted to say pinched there, written right
across her face. He was enjoying this.

'I have disappointed you, Ms Quinn?'

'No.' The reply was too quick, too vehement. 'Why would I be disappointed when
I never thought you were perfect in the first
place?'

Ha—good reply! The more this woman refused to be lured by him, the more interested
he became. He leaned back in his seat, cross-
ing one leg over the other at the knee. 'I can
see I need to be careful not to underestimate
you, Ms Quinn.'

'Are you in the habit of underestimating
women?' Quick as a flash she struck back.
Clever.

'No, I do not underestimate women. I very
much admire them.'

'And they you, it seems.'

Leo gave a self-deprecating shrug.

'Would you say you were an honourable

man, Signor Ravenino?' Her eyebrows disappeared under her fringe.

'I would.'

'Only I happened to be waiting in the reception of Raven Enterprises this afternoon when Vogue Monroe showed up.'

Ah, so this was where she was going. Leo sat forward again. He had been right to caution himself for underestimating her. Despite her innocent looks, she was a journalist after all, and a sharp one.

'That was…unfortunate.' The goading look in Emma's eyes made him elaborate, even though he knew he shouldn't. 'But women I date know the rules. If they choose to ignore them, that's up to them.'

'So you make all the rules?'

'Yes.' He sat back. 'Do you have a problem with that?'

'It's not my job to have an opinion of you. Merely to ascertain the facts.'

But her opinion was there all right, held in the wide, accusatory gaze. Well, so be it. It didn't matter what she thought of him. But it did matter what she put in this article she was writing.

'Your job, as I understood it, was to find out about Raven Enterprises' investment in renewable energy. I wasn't aware it extended to an examination of my morals.'

'It doesn't.' Flustered, she hurried to put him straight. To emphasise the point, she laid her notepad and pen down on the table.

'As long as we are both clear on this matter. I should hate there to be any misunderstanding about what I agreed to in terms of the content of the interview.'

'No, there's no misunderstanding.'

'Bene.' He gave her a polite smile. 'Then perhaps our interview is concluded?'

'Yes, of course. And thank you.'

He rose with her, watching as she put on her jacket, fastening the one button across her waist.

'How will you get home?'

'Oh, I'll get the night tube.'

'It's too late to be using public transport. My driver will take you home. In fact…' he warmed to his theme '…why don't I drive you myself? In one of my *flashy* cars.'

His pointed use of her phrase was acknowledged with an upward glance.

'No, really, that won't be necessary.'

'I insist. I like driving round big cities at night. It would be my pleasure.'

His arm went loosely around her waist to

guide her forward before she could argue any more. For some reason he wasn't quite ready to bid farewell to this woman yet.

CHAPTER THREE

As the car cruised along the banks of the Thames, Leo stole a glance at his passenger. The postcode he'd entered into the satnav indicated an area way out to the north, somewhere he had never ventured.

His knowledge of London was pretty much limited to the City, the West End and the affluent areas where the privileged few lived in beautiful Georgian terraces or penthouse apartments. He owned neither, preferring to stay in a hotel when he visited the city. It made life less complicated. He had quite enough complications as it was.

His new life, the one he had carved out for himself when the old one had so spectacularly imploded, was crazy busy. His focus had been all consuming, his determination to create a multi-billion-dollar business empire in the shortest time possible driving him ruthlessly on. And he had succeeded. In three short years Raven Enterprises had become hugely successful, and Leo Ravenino one of the most highly respected businessmen in the world.

Described as the man with the Midas touch, his uncanny ability to seek out start-up companies and then have the courage to back them when more experienced traders considered them far too speculative had earned him the reputation of a reckless trailblazer. Leo himself put his success down to hard graft and meticulous research. Though even he had to admit luck had played its part, particularly when his frequent trips to the casinos failed to put a dent in his fortune.

But quite frankly he was due some luck.

'So, are you a Londoner, Emma?' He rested his hands on the wheel, enjoying the smooth feel of the leather, the soft purr of the engine.

'No.' She had a low voice, smooth, sexy. 'But I've been living here for eight years.'

'Where are you from originally?'

'Um…the West Country.' Deliberately vague. Something about her reticence made him want to dig deeper.

'So you came to London to find fame and fortune?'

'Not exactly.' She gave a short laugh. 'More to start a new life.'

Interesting. Leo kept his eyes on the road ahead, waiting for her to elaborate, but she remained stubbornly silent.

'Did you always want a career in journalism?'

'I like writing, particularly research-based information. I thought about doing a history degree to start with, then decided I'd stand a better chance of getting a good job if I went in for journalism.'

'Even so, I imagine it's a competitive world, isn't it?' Tough too. She looked too innocent to be competing with the hardnosed hacks he'd come across. But he'd already caught a glimpse of steel behind the wide blue eyes. He already knew she was clever.

'Yes, it is.'

'So you have done well to secure a position at the *Paladin*?'

'Yes.' He briefly sensed her pride before she checked herself. 'Though I have to confess this is the first solo interview I've done. Up until now I've been mostly shadowing the features editor, checking facts, writing up his pieces for him.'

'Which explains why you were so determined it shouldn't be cancelled.'

'Yes.' He finally heard her smile. 'There

was no way I could go back to Don saying I'd failed.'

'Then I'm sorry I made it difficult for you.'

'That's okay.' She turned to him. 'We got there in the end.'

Leo stopped the car at a red light. It was a warm night so he lowered the window, resting his arm on the sill as he gazed at the near empty streets. A small group of people was clustered around a kebab van on the corner.

'Are you hungry, by any chance?' He turned back to his companion.

'No!' That startled negative again, just when she had been starting to thaw.

'Do you mind if I get one?'

Pulling the car over, he sauntered across to join the short queue. Looking back, he could see Emma's outline in the passenger seat, just make out that she had pulled down the visor to check her reflection in the mirror. So not totally without vanity. And not totally impervious to him. The thought pleased him and as he gave his order to the proprietor, a large gentleman wielding a lethal-looking serrated blade, he decided Ms Emma Quinn was his challenge. He would find a way to break through that prim exterior even if it took all night. It was a surprisingly tempting thought.

* * *

Emma had no idea how she had ended up sitting on a bench on the bank of the Thames at two o'clock in the morning with a handsome Italian billionaire by her side, but somehow she had.

The kebabs had been eaten watching the wide, dark river snake its way past. Despite her saying no, Leo had come back with two polystyrene boxes, handing her one in such a way it would have been churlish to refuse. And all pretence of not being hungry had vanished with the first bite. She was starving.

Conversation between them picked up between mouthfuls, being outside, cocooned in the dim light, doing something as ordinary as eating a kebab breaking down the barriers between them until Emma felt herself start to relax. More than that, she felt happy. Leo, too, appeared to be at ease. Not the practised, urbane charm he had shown her in the club, but a more casual, laid-back style that only made him all the more attractive.

Asking about her job he appeared to be genuinely interested in her replies, following up with inciteful comments, anecdotes of his own. Conversation had flowed easily, from her favourite places in London to whether she liked chilli sauce. Musings about how deep the Thames was, where pigeons went to sleep. Safe, silly things.

Leo was clever, quick-witted, good company. He made her laugh. And he also made her tingle with desire. All over. Everywhere. From the top of her scalp to the tips of her toes. Like she had been electrified. Like he only had to touch her and a bolt of light would fizz between them. Somehow his inherent sexiness had infiltrated her veins like a silent assassin.

'It's a clear night tonight.' Running his arm along the back of the bench behind her, Leo tipped his head back to look at the sky. An hour had passed and still neither of them had made any attempt to move.

'Yes.' Emma copied him, her head thrown back. 'I love looking up at the stars. As a child I tried to learn the different constellations.'

'Then here is your challenge, Ms Quinn.' He moved closer. 'What can you see up there?'

'Well, there's a lot of light pollution...'

'No excuses.'

'Okay!' Emma laughed. 'Well, there's the Big Dipper, right overhead. Though technically it's not a constellation, just part of Ursa Major, the Great Bear. If you follow the handle towards the southwest, the next star you meet is Arcturus.'

'Fascinating.'

'And beyond that Corona Borealis.'

'Did anyone ever tell you that you have a beautiful neck?'

'N-no.' Emma stopped breathing, her head still thrown back, her heart racing.

'And I should very much like to kiss it.' So close now, his breath felt like the flutter of a bird's wing against her skin.

There was a second's stillness and then his lips were at the base of her throat, hot and damp, gentle yet firm. Emma's eyes closed, pinpricks of desire shooting through her body, all over, everywhere. Slowly, almost imperceptibly his mouth moved up her neck, goosebumps trailing in its wake, the brush of his hair another, exquisite torture. At the base of her ear he stopped, pulling back, waiting. Emma opened her eyes. The stars were still above her. Very slowly she raised her head. Their eyes met. Leo's dark head moved closer. And then his mouth was on hers.

Sensations detonated in her head, elation flooding every part of her body. Tingling, clenching, twitching feelings, assaulting her nerve endings, affecting all of her. *So this was what a kiss could be like.* Something extraordinary. Something that made you feel things you'd never felt before, leaving you reaching for an unknown that you couldn't quite grasp, yearning for something you had never even known existed until that moment, but which now seemed vitally important. Hanging on to the yearning sensation, refusing to let it slip away, because that, too, was beautiful in its own right. Affecting, astonishing.

On a shared gasp of breath, they pulled apart, just enough to find each other's eyes. Leo's fingers gently threaded through her hair, cradling her head, the swelling silence holding them still but offering no answers. A swallow moved the column of his throat and for a moment it looked as if he was going to speak. But instead he angled his head until his lips were on hers again.

An explosion ripped through Emma once more, her neural pathways ready for him this time, like following the flattened track through a field of corn. Her arms went around his neck, registering the heat of him, the form of his shoulders, broad and strong, the powerful, sleeping strength. Beneath closed lids she let herself drift without thinking, take without question, give without shyness. She let herself go.

Leo's arms strayed to her waist, and then

they were both standing, the kiss still hard and hungry, Leo leaning in to her until she could feel all of him beneath his clothes, hard planes, jutting bones, warm skin stretched over bunched muscles. And the unmistakable swell of arousal pressing against her stomach. Emma edged closer, seeking more, her hands shaking until she linked them behind Leo's head, pressing as tightly as she could to make them stop, to prevent her whole body from convulsing. Even if that felt like heaven too.

'Emma?' Her name on his lips was both a question and a promise. A search for truth wrapped in a quiet dare.

He waited, but when met only with Emma's thrumming silence he continued anyway. 'My hotel is not far from here.'

Emma swallowed, the frantic pulse of her blood acknowledging exactly what he was saying, the pound of her heart repeating it over and over. Dragging her eyes away from Leo's black gaze, she took a step back until Leo's arms dropped down by his sides. She looked down at herself, expecting to be somehow changed, altered by what had just happened. By the tumult still coursing through her. But, no, she looked exactly the same, the plain navy suit still stopping demurely at her knee, the jacket buttoned at the waist giving no sign of the tumult beneath—breasts swollen with heat, skin pulled tight, nipples hardened peaks. No visible sign of the pulsing ache that was gripping her core.

She turned her head, making herself focus on the wide pavement in front of them, the ornate streetlights, and beyond that the river, quiet and dark.

Leo Ravenino was dangerous—she knew that. His reputation went before him, she had seen the evidence for herself. Vogue Monroe's outburst in the foyer of Raven Enterprises a classic example of a woman scorned. The stories Nathalie had told her only confirming everything she'd thought she knew. In affairs of the heart, Leo Ravenino was a dark and lethal force.

But forewarned was forearmed. Emma tried to order her thoughts. She knew exactly what Leo was offering. She also knew with every sensible, practical bone in her body that she should turn him down. And before that kiss she would have done. No question. Even though Leo's seduction had been in the air all evening, it had been sufficiently subtle, casual for Emma to ignore. She had just assumed he was programmed to do it; part of who he was.

And equally she was programmed to

repel such advances. Not for nothing had she earned the nickname *Ice Quinn* by the teenage boys who had found their advances swiftly rebuffed when she'd been younger. A moniker that had lodged in her brain all this time.

But she didn't feel like an ice queen now. She felt heat in every part of her body, every cell jumping with excitement. She felt a recklessness urging her on, ordering her to take this chance. Sucking in her kiss-swollen lips, she waited for sanity to kick in, for her rational voice to finally pipe up and tell her to primly decline Leo's offer and ask to be driven home. It was what she would have sworn her reply would be if you had asked her at the start of the evening. And yet...still that voice didn't come. Instead there was another one clamouring for her to take this opportunity, to step out of her straitjacket and live life for the moment for once.

Watching those dancers in the nightclub, their bodies so fluid and loose, so uninhibited, had made her see how tightly she was strung. Back then, held in Leo's arms, she had been rigid with tension. But not now. Suddenly one night of reckless indulgence seemed overwhelmingly tempting. One night when she threw off the shackles of responsibility and stopped being so damned sensible, just living for the moment, impossible to resist. One night when she let herself go to see what would happen.

Leo was waiting for her answer, the patient silence belied by his heated stare. Eyes that shone as black as night. Under the streetlight his short, dark hair gleamed richly, shadowed hollows shaping his face. The air was thick with the pull of his magnetism, but he made no move to touch her again, to influence her decision with another bruising kiss. Instead an old-fashioned courtesy prevailed, a quiet respectfulness she hadn't expected of him. Sure, there was an arrogance in the way he held himself, an inbuilt confidence, but it was clear that the decision was hers and hers alone.

And Emma knew she had already made it. She swallowed hard, flashing Leo a smile that arrowed straight to his groin. 'Let's go.'

Finally letting the air out of his lungs, Leo felt for Emma's hand, holding it tightly in his, as if to bind her to him. Waiting for her to make her decision had tested him to breaking point. With rampant impatience firing every cell of his body, he'd had to harness all his self-control not to make the decision for her, in the form of another blazing kiss. But somehow he had managed to restrain himself and now the wait was over. Almost.

They were only ten minutes from his hotel. He could last that long. He took in a breath that did nothing to calm his libido, both fascinated and shocked by the extraordinary effect she was having on him. What had started as a mild attraction had rapidly morphed into a desperate need. He wanted Emma more than he had wanted any woman in a very long time.

With unseemly haste he led them back to his car. Ten minutes, he told himself. That's all. Opening the door for Emma, he waited, expecting her to slide inside, but instead she turned to face him, tilting her face up to his, her expression hard to read in the low light. Solemn, thoughtful, but still as sexy as hell. She had changed her mind, was that it? Leo braced himself for the crushing news that he would be taking her home, chastely dropping her at her door.

But instead her arms wound around his neck, lowering his head until it met hers. A fresh bolt of arousal jerked through him as she started to kiss him, tentative at first, but then long and deep, full of hunger. Dio, *what was she trying to do to him?* His hands felt for the button of her jacket, sliding beneath to the silky shirt, over the gorgeous swell of her breasts, nipples tightening beneath his touch. He wanted more. So much more. He longed to feel those curves beneath his fingertips, to make her tremble beneath his caress. But not here, like this.

Urgency fuelling every movement, he got them both in the car, the roar of the engine echoing the roar in his blood as he navigated the empty roads back to his hotel in a silence that thrummed with need. Chucking the car keys to the doorman, he hurried Emma inside, their footsteps echoing across the marble lobby, their lips meeting as the elevator doors slid closed, still locked when they opened again.

Clasped in each other's arms, they half stumbled in the direction of the bedroom, tripping over each other, laughing at their eagerness, the madness of what they were doing, the heat of their breath flushing their faces, the hammering of their hearts loud enough to feel. But no words. Words were superfluous.

Arriving at his bed in a tangle of twisted clothes and eager limbs, Leo took a moment to stare down at Emma. So beautiful. How had he not noticed it right from the start? Wide eyes, full lips, her shoulder-length brown hair spread out on the pillow. The jacket already gone, now he undid the buttons of her blouse as slowly as his desire would let him, moving the fabric to expose her bra, the swell of her breasts. His breath was as hot as fire as his tongue found the valley of her cleavage, dipping down as low as he could reach. Her soft moan drove him on, matched by a groan of his own as she reached behind to undo her bra, shrugging it off along with her blouse.

Leaving her just long enough to rip off his clothes, Leo reached for a condom packet, impatiently ripping it open with his teeth. By the time he was back, Emma was naked, her arms above her head, stretching her breasts, her legs together, writhing gently as they twisted around one another.

Leo had never seen such a beautiful sight. His urge to take her more extreme, more mind-numbingly vital than anything he had ever felt before.

Gazing into the shadows of Leo's face, Emma tried to capture the moment, knowing she was about to be changed for ever. Dilated pupils, a jaw set hard with concentration, mouth pulled tight now, like he was teetering on the edge. Like he meant to own all of her. *She had done this to him.*

Winding her arms around his neck, she threaded her fingers in his hair, pulling him down to kiss her again. His mouth came down on hers, feverish and crushing, mind numbing. *This was it.* She arched up to meet him, her breath stolen as Leo lowered himself down, skin on skin, the jut of his hips hard against her own, the solid weight of his erection pressing against the sweet, damp fire of her core.

'Cosi bella.' He rasped the words as he nudged himself against the aching folds, a throbbing shudder of pleasure pulsing through her. 'So beautiful.'

Then he was inside her, thrusting hard and deep, the cry she let out making him hesitate until she wrapped her legs around his back, urging him on as she started to convulse ecstatically around the length of him.

And all rational thought was instantly obliterated.

CHAPTER FOUR

THERE WAS SOMETHING about her head on the pillow, the untidy curtain of hair, a solemnity held in her features, even in sleep. Leo allowed himself to stare, just for a few moments. But not with pleasure. And certainly not with any sense of satisfaction. Far from it. His overriding emotion was guilt.

He watched as her eyes fluttered beneath closed lids so delicate he could make out the tiny blue veins. Her mouth twitched. The mouth that had felt so good beneath his own, that he had encouraged to explore his body, to touch and taste, leaving him shuddering with pleasure beneath its featherlike stroke. But not there…at least he had held back from that, even though she had wanted to. At least he didn't have that first on his conscience.

Who was he kidding? His conscience had no place to hide. In the cold light of this grey London morning he had to face the facts.

Emma had been a virgin. He had taken something from her that she could never get back. He hadn't known, not until the last moment, but even then it wouldn't have been too late. He could have stopped. He *should* have stopped. Despite Emma urging him on, he should have found the willpower to pull back, to say no, to wrench himself from temptation. *Such temptation.*

But instead he had greedily taken her soft assurances at face value, firmly ignored the voice in his head telling him this was wrong. And not just once. But repeatedly. All night long, in fact. Her generous, giving body obsessing him in a way he had never experienced before. And the more she gave the more he took. After all, there was no going back now, so what difference would it make? What was done was done.

But now he saw that twisted logic for what it was. The selfish and greedy actions of a man who thought of no one but himself. The man he had become. Somewhere along the line his power and success had taken him down a path to a place he no longer liked, turned him into a man he no longer respected. Dating a succession of beautiful high-profile women, just because he could, no longer felt like any sort of achievement, just fatuous vanity.

As Emma stirred beneath his scrutiny, Leo felt his lip curl in self-disgust. This rare woman deserved someone so much better than him. Taking one last look, he turned away, walked quietly through the suite of rooms, picking up his belongings as he went. This he could do for her. Get out of her life before he messed it up any further. A clean break. She deserved nothing less.

'These came for you.' Don, the features editor, appeared from behind an enormous bunch of flowers. 'Seems like you made quite an impression on someone.'

By 'someone' it was clear he knew perfectly well who. A blush staining her cheeks, Emma took them from him, laying them down heavily on top of the papers on her cluttered desk.

'No need to look like that.' Don gave a short laugh. 'How you choose to do your research is up to you. But I'll be expecting a great article.' His wink as he turned to go only mortified Emma still further. 'End of the day, okay?'

Emma cleared her throat. 'Yes, sure.'

She made herself look at the flowers, her

stomach twisting. *It was exactly the same bunch he had sent Vogue Monroe*. The innocent bouquet stared back at her like an insult. So, this was how little last night had meant to him. How little she had meant. Despite the sick feeling in her gut, she still found her fingers parting the blooms, looking for a note, looking for some confirmation, no matter how small, that she had got it wrong. That the closeness they had shared had been special. Not just for her but for him too.

But there was nothing. *He has the florist on speed dial*. Nathalie's comment came back to haunt her. No doubt the work of seconds, she had been dealt with, dismissed, forgotten.

Not that she was surprised. Waking up alone in Leo's hotel suite had sent a very clear message. Realising he had gone without even saying goodbye had hurt. A lot. But what had she expected? Sweet nothings and clasped hands over a leisurely breakfast? Promises that they should keep in touch, that he would look her up next time he was in London? That wasn't Leo Ravenino's style, and Emma knew it.

But that hadn't prevented the hollowness inside, an emptiness that had only seemed to expand as she had hurried home, showering and dressing, the same as she did every day.

Taking the underground into work, nodding good morning to her colleagues as usual, sitting at her desk, preparing to start work.

Reading through her interview notes, it felt like they had been written an age ago, by someone else entirely. But the recording on her phone remained unplayed. Emma wasn't ready to hear his voice again. It was too personal, too *him*. If she was going to hold it together today, she had to blot out everything that had happened last night and concentrate firmly on the article she had to write.

And up until now she had succeeded. It had been a struggle but keeping her head down and all her focus on work, she had managed to get the first five hundred words done. Concise, informative, impartial, a quick readthrough confirmed she had done a good job. And she still had plenty of time to finish it. But the arrival of the wretched flowers had derailed her. The fragile hold on her concentration gone, the enormity of what she had done last night reared up, filling her mind. Stealing the words she wanted to write.

It wasn't like she regretted it exactly. How could she regret something so amazing, so *altering*? It was more that she felt cut adrift, like she didn't know who she was any more. Yesterday she would have sworn she would never get involved with a man like Leonardo Ravenino, that the idea of going back to his hotel and spending the night with him was inconceivable. And yet she had. Willingly. Urgently. Giving herself freely, taking greedily.

She felt somehow duped by her own self. And she felt annoyed that she had succumbed to Leo's practised seduction the same way so many other women had in the past, and no doubt would in the future. She had imagined herself cleverer than that, sharper. Now she knew she wasn't. As the pretty blooms by her side made all too clear.

She picked up the bouquet, steadying the weight with her hand. She would just get rid of them, that was the answer. Emma looked around her. They were too big to dump straight in the bin and offering them to someone else would only provoke questions and she couldn't bear that. So instead she shoved them under her desk as best she could, deciding she would deal with them later. Drawing in her chair, she turned to her article again.

But it was no good, the right words refused to come. Instead of his business affairs all she could think of was Leo the lover. Fevered thoughts tumbled over each other, fighting for centre stage. The stories in the tabloid press, the things she had heard from Nathalie, the look on Vogue Monroe's face… What was it she had called him? *A selfish, arrogant, egotistical bastard.* And this was the man she had chosen to lose her virginity to. The first man she had ever wanted. Well, more fool her.

She had never viewed her virginity as some sort of prize, more a sort of mothballed corner, one she wasn't sure she would ever expose to the light. The succession of men coming and going in her mother's life, and hers, too, by default, had firmly put her off casual relationships. The last one, in particular, had put her off both sex and men in general. The trauma of that incident had definitely left its mark.

So when no one she ever met even tempted her to change her mind, Emma had decided maybe that was it. She really was the Ice Quinn. She was too cold or too scarred or somehow wired the wrong way to ever want to have sex. Celibacy was fine. From what she could see of other people's messed-up relationships, she was better off staying single anyway.

But meeting Leo altered everything. She had been completely swamped by the power of the attraction. Drowned by it. Drugged by it. It didn't justify what she had done, or make her action remotely more sensible or acceptable, but it was the best explanation she could come up with.

Emma stared at her computer screen, her hand on the mouse opening up a blank page almost before she realised it. The written word had always been her refuge. Part of a chaotic and largely dysfunctional family, her way of coping had been to take herself off, to write down her worries and fears, her frustrations and anxieties, commit them to pages in a notebook in all their funny, febrile or furious glory, depending on what was inside her head at the time. And then she would destroy them. Because just the act of writing the words made her feel better, it released the pressure in her head.

Tentatively, her fingers touched the keyboard. Maybe this would be a way to vent her feelings, to take away the drilling in her head, the annoying ache inside. For her eyes only, she could write a no-holds-barred exposé of the life and loves of Leo Ravenino. Get it all out. Then maybe she would be able to concentrate on the piece she was supposed to be writing.

Inside the world of Leo Ravenino: the life and loves of a billionaire Latin playboy!

The headline wrote itself. And before long her fingers were flying over the keyboard.

Che diamine! What the hell…?

Leo stared at the article in horror. No, it couldn't have been written by her. It wasn't possible. But there was the byline, clearly written beneath the offending title: *by Emma Quinn.*

He threw the newspaper down in disgust, anger coursing through him, rushing through his veins as he thought back to the interview, to what had happened afterwards. To the woman he had thought she was.

Snatching the paper back up, he scanned the article again, the words jumping out at him like knives. Details of his private life laid out for all to see. Personal, intimate things, painting him like a heartless philanderer, some kind of lascivious monster. The sort of man no woman was safe to be around.

> *Breaking the heart of a British socialite after she had told her family they would shortly be wed.*
> *Abandoning an Italian heiress on his yacht in the South of France when she refused to accept that their relationship was over.*

Expecting his staff to deal with hysterical ex-lovers turning up at his offices.

Leo's hands curled into fists. How dared she…? And not content with raking over his private life, exposing his misdemeanours for all to see, there were the comments about his background. Questions posed about the principality of Ravenino, the ending of his engagement, the reason for his rapid departure.

Was his ex-fiancé yet another victim of this cold-hearted lover?
Or perhaps the responsibility of running a principality was just too arduous a life for this Latin playboy?

Leo dragged in a breath of fire that scorched right through his lungs. How the hell could he have got this woman so wrong? He, who prided himself on his intuition, his ability to read people so well, had been totally fooled by this Emma Quinn. Totally fooled by her guileless 'innocence'. To think he had actually felt guilty for the way he had treated her! Agonised over taking her virginity. Now he saw her for what she was. A ruthless opportunist who had been prepared to trade her virginity for a scoop. For the sake of a tawdry newspaper article.

Well, she would soon realise her mistake. No one double-crossed Leonardo Ravenino and got away with it. Reaching for his phone, he quickly found the number he was looking for and pressed dial. Emma Quinn's precious career at the *Paladin* was just about to come to an end. He would make sure of it.

'Well, this is one hell of a mess.' Don raked a hand through his hair, his eyes, when they finally met hers, heavy with defeat. 'I hold myself partly responsible for not checking the article, but ultimately it's you he wants gone.'

'Gone?' Emma repeated the word faintly.

'Yep. He was quite explicit. Either you quit, forthwith, or he's going to sue the *Paladin*. And, quite frankly, we wouldn't have a leg to stand on. Not when we are faced with this…' He gestured to the newspaper spread out on the desk before him, folded back to the features page, where Emma's article stared back at them in all its black and white horror. A wave of sickness passed over her again.

Writing in the heat of the moment, with a churn of emotions going round in her head, she had not held back. She had poured everything into it, adopting classic tabloid language to spell out a torrid mix of truths and rumour about Leo Ravenino's many love affairs, his callous treatment of the women, his lack of morals, his egotism, the ruthless streak behind the urbane charm, on and on. For good measure she had even chucked in some speculation about his past, pointedly wondering what exactly had happened to make him leave Ravenino in such a hurry, why the title had never been passed down to him.

It was an explosive bomb of a piece, the fragments flying far and wide. *But it was never meant to be published.*

Emma slumped in the chair opposite Don, her elbows on her knees, her head in her hands. Like some sort of dreadful nightmare, she kept hoping she would wake up. That Don hadn't hurried over to her desk the day before, saying he had just heard they needed the piece on Ravenino right away. That she hadn't rushed to finish it in a terrible panic, her head still all over the place, lack of sleep mushing her brain. That she hadn't clicked 'send' without checking what she was doing…

She had only found out she'd filed the wrong article this morning. Hauled into the office at first light, she had been met by Don's horrified face holding the newspaper before him like a weapon of mass destruction. Which it was really. The destruction of her career.

'Is there nothing we can do? I can do?' She raised her head, searching for a flicker of hope. But Don's bleak expression made it clear there was no hope to be had.

'I'm sorry, lass.' He reached for her hand. 'You're a good writer and we'll make a journalist out of you yet. But there is no going back from a mistake like this. Ravenino wants your blood and the *Paladin* is going to make sure he gets it.'

CHAPTER FIVE

Two months later

SHIELDING HER EYES from the sun, Emma gazed up at the headquarters of Raven Enterprises. Located in the heart of Milan's business district, it was the tallest, most imposing building of all, a gleaming metal tower of post-modernist construction. She returned her gaze to the pavement, focussing on steadying the thump of her heart.

She hadn't made an appointment, knowing full well that any request to see Leo would have been denied without a detailed explanation. And that explanation needed to be made face to face. But now she risked being refused entry. Parallels with Vogue Monroe in London flashed through her mind. At the time she had felt sorry for Vogue, but she had only lost her boyfriend, her pride, maybe a little bit of her heart. In comparison, Emma had lost everything.

But luck, if you could call it that, was with her today. The revolving doors turned, and two men stood on the pavement, speaking in rapid Italian, shaking hands.

Emma's stomach swooped.

'*Guardero le figure e ti farò sapere. Ti prego di tenere questo tra noi.*'

There was an exchange of farewells before the taller man turned back. And suddenly his slate-grey eyes were on hers. Shock flitted across his face, his jaw visibly hardening, his senses on high alert.

'Ms Quinn.'

Nothing more, just that. Her name on his lips like a curse. His gaze aimed like a weapon.

'Leo.' Emma tried to match his tone. She had prepared hard for this moment. She wasn't here to try and justify herself, to make friends, even if that were possible, which she knew it wasn't. She was here to say what needed to be said and then leave. She had to be calm and logical. Keep her emotions at bay.

Who was she kidding? There was nothing calm or logical about the visceral impact of seeing him again. It was hot and hard and terrifyingly real. Just one glance at him had seen her emotions detonate like a bomb inside her. She mentally amended her objectives: she needed to keep her emotions hidden.

'There is something I have to speak to you about.' She choked out the words on a dry breath.

Leo closed the space between them with a couple of lethal strides, his eyes never leaving her face.

'Something so important that it brings you to Milan?' Suspicion furrowed his brow, narrowed his eyes.

'Yes.'

A fleeting look of unease crossed his face before it was banished by command. 'Very well.'

Taking her elbow, he turned Emma around, issuing rapid instructions to a receptionist as he marched them through the foyer towards an elevator. As they were whisked noiselessly skyward, he made no attempt to speak to her, the silence an almost palpable indictment in itself.

'Follow me.'

He led her down a wide corridor, touching his finger to a keypad to usher her into a huge glass office with windows on all sides, a panoramic view of Milan in every direction. Following Leo towards his desk, Emma concentrated on putting one foot in front of the other, looking neither left nor right. She was feeling queasy enough already, without vertigo kicking in. Pulling out a seat for her, Leo moved to the other side of the desk.

'Go ahead.' Wasting no time, he fixed her with sharp grey eyes. With his elbows resting on the desk, his fingers, Emma noticed, had threaded together to make a fist. 'Say whatever it is you have to say.'

Emma swallowed hard. His tone was harsh, his cold demeanour not making this any easier. But, then, what did she expect?

'I'm sorry...' she hesitated. 'About the article I wrote.'

She hadn't meant to start with this, or maybe even mention it at all. It felt as if years had passed since her stupid mistake, rather than a couple of months. Events since had overtaken it, overtaken her, skewing time. But faced with Leo again, his blatant hostility, she knew she should apologise. And she had to do it now, before the maelstrom of what was to come took away this chance.

'You have come all this way to tell me that?' Distaste coloured his words. 'Because, if so, you have had a wasted journey. I neither need nor want your apology.'

'But you are going to hear it anyway.' Her voice was low but determined. Leo might not want to hear what she had to say but she was still going to say it. Even if it was just to salve her own conscience.

'I made a mistake, Leo. That article was never meant to be published.'

'No?' Sarcasm scored his voice. 'So how come it ended up splashed all over the newspaper?'

'Because I filed the wrong copy.'

'You lied to me, Ms Quinn. You lied about the subject of our interview. All along you intended to produce that grubby little exposé.'

'No, it wasn't like that, truly.' Emma sat forward. 'I wrote that piece solely for myself. I was trying to make sense of what had happened…between us… I was confused and muddled… No one was meant to see it.'

'You expect me to believe that?'

'It's the truth, Leo.' She lowered her voice.

A bruised silence stretched between them. Emma looked down at her clasped hands.

'Well, either way, a vicious concoction of half-truths and fictitious garbage was written by you and printed in a national newspaper for the world to see.'

Emma winced. It was true, she couldn't deny it.

'The *Paladin* did issue an apology.' It was a feeble defence as his dismissive huff made clear.

'I just hope you felt better after you had got that off your chest.'

'Of course I didn't feel better.' Heat bloomed on her skin. 'I felt terrible. I lost my job. You made sure of that.'

'And are you surprised?'

No, she hadn't been surprised, not really. She had made a dreadful blunder.

'You are lucky I didn't personally sue you for slander.'

But she didn't feel lucky. Not at all. At the time losing her job had felt like the biggest calamity that could ever befall her. Now she knew it was just the start of her troubles.

A couple of seconds passed. Leo picked up a pen, tapping it on the desk.

'If that is all you came to say, I believe our business is concluded.'

'No.' Emma's stomach tightened. If only it were that straightforward. 'That is not all I came to say. There is another matter we need to discuss.'

'Go on.'

The weight of his gaze felt heavy enough to flatten her, every nerve-filled second dragging longer than the last. She took a brave breath.

'I am pregnant.' The words felt like boulders in her mouth, too big, too unruly. 'I am going to have a baby.'

Like a predator surprised by his prey, Leo remained perfectly still, his entire focus trained on her. Light played over the dark sheen of his hair, emphasising the stark angles of his face. His silence was total, torturous.

'I thought you should know.'

He rose from his chair suddenly, sending it flying behind him. Turning his back to her, he moved towards the window, feet planted apart, his broad shoulders set in a menacing line, silence following in his wake. 'And you are telling me this because...?' Addressing the view, his voice rang with measured authority.

'Because you are the father, of course.'

That silence again, before he slowly turned. His gaze, when it met hers, fierce enough to leave marks. Emma refused to blink, refused to swallow. She was not going to be cowed.

'And why should I believe you? After all...' his voice dropped to an almost conversational burr '...you have done nothing but lie to me since the moment we met.'

'I made a mistake and I have apologised for it.' Emma felt her nails dig into her palms. 'But, trust me, on this matter there is no mistake. You are the father.'

'And how can you be so sure?'

Deep breaths, Emma, deep breaths.

'Because I have never slept with anyone else.' She spoke slowly, deliberately, scratching around for every bit of control she possessed. 'You are the only person I have ever had sex with.'

Leo forced his lungs to start working, his mind scrabbling to take in this shocking news. *Pregnant.* Was that possible? He had used a condom every time they had made love, hadn't he? *Every time?* Now his tortured mind tried to recall, he couldn't be one hundred per cent sure. How many times had he taken her that night? His desire refusing to be sated, sleep evading him in favour of nestling up against her soft curves, sliding his hands between her thighs, pressing the hard length of him against her back, hooking his leg over her hip. And every time she had responded he had experienced the same surge of exhilaration, the thrill of possessing her anew never diminishing. Something about the sweetly naive way she had given herself to him had called to his most basic instincts.

If he'd had a cave, he would have slung her over his shoulder and carried her off there, made her his and his alone.

But he didn't have a cave, just a ridiculously huge penthouse hotel suite. And in the morning, when he had realised his mistake, berating himself for taking advantage of such an innocent, he had left. For her own good. The flowers had been an ill-judged afterthought when the memory of her had plagued him throughout the day.

The irony was that while he was being racked with guilt, agonising over his behaviour, even whether or not he should have sent her flowers, Emma Quinn had been doing a hatchet job on him. Writing a vicious exposé that the most seasoned tabloid hack would have been proud of. Maybe she *had* submitted that article by mistake. He didn't care. None of that mattered any more. Except he now had an insight into exactly what she thought of him. Which could prove useful for future negotiations.

Seeing her standing there outside Raven Enterprises, all wide eyes beneath that brown fringe, had sent a bolt of shock right through him. Like he had conjured her up just by thinking about her. Because he *had* thought about her, way too much. Not only that, but his usual appetite for female company had deserted him. He had told himself it was all about pride. Being duped by Emma Quinn had made him question his judgement. It was no wonder he was in no rush to date again. No wonder he couldn't get the woman out of his mind.

And now here she was, back again. Ready to rock the very foundations of his carefully constructed world. Not with some stupid article, that seemed insignificant now. But with a pregnancy. A baby. His child.

If it was true. Leo sat down again. He needed to think this through calmly. Who was to say she was really pregnant? He already knew he couldn't trust her. This might be some scam to try and get money out of him. And even if she was, the baby wasn't necessarily his. Denial started to force its way to the surface. She could have hooked up with anyone in the past few weeks, found she was pregnant, then decided to say it was his because of his wealth. He had no idea what she was capable of. After all, he barely knew her, as he had discovered to his cost.

And hadn't he himself been the victim of just such heinous subterfuge? His own mother had concealed from her husband the true paternity of her elder son, to further her own ends. Leo had no intention of being taken in by Emma Quinn the way Alberto had been tricked by his mother.

Fixing her with a punishing stare, he hardened his voice.

'You will forgive me if I need further proof.' She didn't look as if she would forgive him. She looked like she wanted to hit him over the head with something hard and sharp. 'How do I know you are pregnant? You might be making the whole thing up.'

There was a brief, angry silence. 'And why on earth would I do that?'

Leo had to admit she did look genuinely nonplussed, as if she had no idea what he was talking about. With flushed cheeks and too-bright eyes, her hair falling over her shoulders, he was forced to remember how attractive she was. But then if you were trying to trick a man into raising a kid that wasn't his, you would make the effort to look appealing. Except she didn't appear to have made any effort. Wearing skinny jeans and a baggy check shirt, well-worn sneakers on her feet, she gave the appearance of someone who had thrown on the first things she could find. So why was he so drawn to her?

He shrugged, affecting an insouciance he

was far from feeling. 'You wouldn't be the first gold-digger out to trap a wealthy man.'

Her look was one of utter disgust, but there was hurt there, too, like she had been verbally slapped. Well, so be it. He knew he sounded cruel, but the brute in him had taken over. If she was messing with him, she needed to be put straight.

'For your information…' she dealt him a vicious stare '… I have no desire to trap any man, least of all an arrogant, narcissistic one like you.'

On her feet now, she picked up her canvas holdall and slung it over the crook of her arm, snatching up her handbag.

'I came here to tell you that you are going to be a father, because, like I said, I thought you had a right to know. If I'd had any idea you would react in such an insulting, barbaric manner, I wouldn't have bothered. But at least I can go back to London with a clear conscience, knowing I have done my duty. And when my child is old enough to ask about his father, I will be sure to tell him, or her, that he was such a paranoid egotist he refused to believe in their existence. Goodbye, Leo. Have a nice life.'

She swung violently around, her bag catching on the arm of her chair, sending it toppling sideways. She hesitated, looking as if she was about to pick it up, then changed her mind and headed towards the door.

'*Aspetta!* Wait!' Leo was behind her in a couple of seconds, his hand on her arm. He could feel the resistance there, but eventually she turned to face him again. And the brute in him started to subside. Because the colour had dramatically drained from her face, her eyes wild. 'Come and sit down. We need to discuss this rationally.'

'If by rationally you mean you insulting me by telling me I am either lying about you being the father or that I have made the whole thing up, then I won't bother, thank you very much.'

'You need to calm yourself.' So did he, come to that. Leo pulled in a breath. 'Getting hysterical is not going to help the situation.'

'And neither is you behaving like a barbarian.' Emma glared at him, making his jaw clench. His composure was wearing dangerously thin.

Picking up her chair, he lowered her into it again, then went back to his position on the other side of the desk. He looked at down at his hands, clasped tight, the knuckles pulled white. This was one hell of a mess. How could he have been so stupidly, recklessly careless?

'Assuming everything you say is correct...' he saw her start to speak but cut her off with a raised hand '...we need to find a way to proceed.' Somehow, he had to minimise the damage. He just didn't know how yet.

Think, Leo. Think.

'You have been to see a doctor?'

She nodded stiffly. 'She confirmed that I was eight weeks pregnant. Nearly nine now. I am booked in for a scan at twelve weeks.'

'Very well.' His decisiveness returned in a crazy rush. 'You will have the scan here in Milan. I will find the best obstetrician.'

She was looking at him with a mixture of surprise and alarm, but he didn't have the capacity to work out what either emotion meant or how he should read them. It made no difference anyway. They would be playing by his rules.

'In the meantime, you will move into my villa.'

Emma raised her chin, all pulled-tight defiance. 'Actually, I plan to return to London, tonight if possible.'

'No, Emma. That won't be happening.' The calm in his voice was getting harder and harder to find.

'You don't get to tell me what to do, Leo. I

came here to tell you that I am pregnant, not to have you take over my life.'

'The fact that you are pregnant means inevitably our lives are going to change.'

'Yes, but—'

'No buts.'

He heard her sigh. Caught the flicker of unease behind the hard blue stare she wanted him to see.

'Leo…' She tried again. 'I think you have misunderstood my motives. I'm not looking for any sort of commitment from you. I'm not asking for anything. Rest assured…' she folded her arms across her chest '… I am quite prepared to raise the child alone if necessary.'

Leo felt his temper inching up by steady degrees. Emma Quinn had a lot to learn about him.

'And you misunderstand me if you think I would ever consider the idea of allowing my child to be raised anywhere other than with me.'

My child. Leo furrowed his brow. Where had that come from? Five minutes ago he had been prepared to deny its very existence, now he wouldn't countenance the idea of it being raised anywhere other than here, with him.

'So you accept the baby is yours?' Her

words, deliberately aimed, were nevertheless spoken gently, inching their way towards a conscience he didn't want them to find.

Leo frowned deeply. '*Sì*, yes, I do.'

Roughly raking a hand through his hair, he let out a breath. Deep down he knew the child was his. He had known right from the start.

His initial stunned disbelief had quickly given way to stark acceptance. And with that had come the compulsion to take control of the situation—right away. Because Leo Ravenino had a reputation for thinking on his feet, making quick decisions and acting upon them. It had stood him in good stead in the world of business. It was his only option now. He had to bring some order to this chaos.

There was a moment of stillness, time holding its breath. It was Emma who eventually broke it.

'We don't need to make any decisions yet.' Her tone was more conciliatory now. 'The baby won't be born for another seven months after all. I can always come back in a few months, or you could come to London?'

'No. You will stay here, in Italy.' He was not going to be beaten on this one. He wasn't sure himself why he was so certain she shouldn't leave the country, only that the more she pushed against it, the more he was determined that she stay in Italy. Close by, where he could keep an eye on her. Before the board got wind of this fiasco and tried to use it against him. Or this woman went to the press. Or disappeared. Or all of these things. Like a spreading stain, he had to contain this situation as fast as he could.

From nowhere, a thought rushed into his head. As obvious as it was startling, it crowded his mind. Leo tried to let it settle, to test how it felt. Tried to work out if he had found the answer or totally lost the plot. Yes, it was the right decision. He allowed his gaze to travel over Emma's heated face, his conviction solidifying. This was the only course of action. *Marriage*. And the sooner the better.

A small chink of light glimmered through the black clouds. By marrying Emma he could keep a close eye on her, make sure there were no more unfortunate disclosures to the press, intentionally or otherwise. And there was another advantage. It would silence his critics on the board. That wretched article in the *Paladin* hadn't gone unnoticed. Comments had been made; whispers heard from behind closed doors. Raven Enterprises was riding high, but confidence in any company could crash as fast as it rose. One wrong deal, one more scandal could see the board members and shareholders start to turn, investors get nervous. News that he had fathered a child would not be well received. But if he were to get married, that was different. Settling down, starting a family, that was exactly what they wanted to hear.

Decision made; Leo just had to work out when to drop his bombshell. And despite everything, a little frisson of satisfaction went through him. Emma Quinn didn't know it yet, but she was about to be made an offer she couldn't refuse.

CHAPTER SIX

EMMA STARED OUT of the window as Villa Magenta finally came into view, the lush green parkland doing nothing to ease the tension gripping her body. Sure, it was beautiful, the golden turreted edifice standing proud against a deep blue sky as her chauffeured car swept her up the long driveway. A fairytale castle, which was very fitting, as none of this felt real.

Cutting short their meeting, Leo had announced in that high-handed, autocratic manner of his that Luigi, his driver, would be taking her to his villa in the country. They had matters to discuss, he had informed her. He would join her there later that evening. Too weary to argue with him any more, Emma had accepted his order. He was right, they did have things to discuss. Perhaps it would be better to spend a few days here to get things settled before she made her escape back to London.

The woman waiting on the steps introduced herself as Maria, Signor Ravenino's housekeeper. Removing Emma's tatty old bag from Luigi's hand, she showed her into a grand salon, all sky-high ceilings and modern chandeliers, and seated her on a designer leather sofa. Their eyes met as Emma thanked her for the proffered glass of water and Emma couldn't help but wonder what this neat Italian woman must think of her, turning up like this out of the blue, dressed in her scruffy jeans and baggy shirt, hair all over the place and wearing not a scrap of make-up. No doubt she was very different from Leo's usual female guests. But Maria was giving nothing away. She was way too professional for that.

Villa Magenta was every bit as beautiful as Emma had imagined. She had read about the sumptuous villa, recently purchased by Leo and completely restored at enormous expense. She had even seen aerial photos. But never had she imagined herself being here, especially under these circumstances—pregnant with the Italian magnate's child. Surreal didn't begin to describe it.

As she wandered from room to room, waiting for Leo to arrive, Emma tried to order her thoughts, bring some clarity to the mad situation she found herself in.

Her decision to come to Italy to tell Leo she was pregnant had not been a difficult one. Every man had the right to know he was going to be a father and every child the right to know his father had at least been informed. Morally it was a no-brainer. And that was how Emma had dealt with it. She had simply come here to state the facts, expecting nothing in return. Because life had taught her that expectation only led to disappointment. The only person she could rely on was herself.

Her own mother had shunned commitment in any form, preferring instead to not tie herself to any one man. Scarred by Emma's father, who had deserted them when Emma had been just a toddler, moving to Ireland and severing all contact, Mary Behenna had decided never to rely on one man for her happiness, instead choosing a succession of casual relationships. And Emma had hated it. Hated the insecurity of having a parade of different men walking in and out of their lives. Hated one man in particular. One thing was for sure, no way was she ever going to subject her own child to such an upbringing. She was determined that her son or daughter would have the stability that she had craved so badly. She just didn't know yet how to achieve it.

By seven p.m. she had driven herself half-crazy trying to figure out the best way forward, what to say to Leo when he finally deigned to show up. When there was still no sign of him by eight o'clock her anxiety had ratcheted up another notch, joined by simmering indignation. Maria had bustled in with a supper tray for her, but Emma had no appetite. Enquiring what time Signor Ravenino was expected home had produced no results, Maria looking slightly nonplussed that Emma thought she might be privy to such information.

Eventually, she decided to go outside and take a walk around the grounds. It was still light, and a beautiful evening. But she had only descended the first few steps when she realised she wasn't alone. Looking over her shoulder, she spotted Luigi lurking behind her.

'*Buonasera...*' Emma spoke uncertainly.

'*Buonasera*,' Luigi replied politely.

She went down the rest of the steps, heading towards the corner of the villa, when she heard the crunch of gravel behind her. Luigi was following her! By the time she had reached the formal gardens he was just a few steps behind. Quickening her pace, Emma darted behind a perfectly sculpted yew hedge, reappearing by a classical fountain, only to find Luigi had beaten her to it. This was getting ridiculous!

She was about to stomp over to him, make it clear that his presence wasn't wanted, that it was downright creepy, when it suddenly occurred to her. Luigi wasn't pursuing her out of some dodgy interest of his own. He was obeying orders. Leo's orders. He had been told to watch over her, make sure she didn't escape. How insulting was that? No, worse than insulting—it was criminal. She was effectively being imprisoned. Well, they would see about that.

Silently seething, Emma turned on her heel, marching back towards the villa and stomping in through the open front door. And straight into a solid wall of tailored suit. Winded, she pulled back, but not before Leo's hands had closed over her shoulders.

'I need to speak to you.' She shrugged off his hands, furious with the way her heart had done a traitorous little leap of welcome. 'Right away.'

'And I you.' Coolly shrugging off his jacket, he handed it to a waiting Maria, issuing some instructions to her in Italian before picking up the leather attaché case at his feet. 'If you would like to come into the salon.'

His arm snaked around Emma's waist to propel her forward and immediately the kiss of his heat through her clothes set her senses on fire. She tried to move away, but Leo stayed infuriatingly close, only letting go once they were in the salon, when he shut the door behind them, put down the attaché case, and crossed to the sideboard.

'Can I fix you a drink?' He spoke over his shoulder.

'No, thank you.' Emma took several steadying breaths while he had his back to her. 'Well, maybe some water.'

She watched in silence as Leo clinked ice into two glasses, filling one with water and the other one with a generous measure of whisky. He came towards her again, handing her a glass.

'Please, sit down.' He gestured to the sofa; his manner polite, relaxed. Not the same man she had left in Milan a few hours before.

Emma reluctantly did as she was told, then wished she hadn't as Leo remained standing before her, assuming a position of power.

'Maria said you hardly touched the meal she brought.' So they had been talking about her behind her back. She started to seethe again.

'I wasn't hungry, okay? And while we are on the subject of your staff…'

'They haven't been treating you well?' The tone of his voice suggested he would be prepared to fire them on the spot. But, then, he was good at that.

'No, it's not that. But what is the meaning of having Luigi follow me around?'

'I gave him instructions to keep an eye on you, that's true.' Leo seated himself on the sofa opposite Emma, placing his glass on the table next to him. 'Is that a problem?'

'Yes, it is!' she fired back. 'I tried to go for a walk around the grounds and he was tracking me like a bloodhound.'

Slowly, deliberately, Leo lifted his glass to take another sip of whisky.

'Under the circumstances, I thought it only prudent to keep track of your whereabouts.'

'Why, what did you think I was going to do?' Heat stained her cheeks. 'Run off with the family silver?'

'There is no family silver.' With tightly reined composure, Leo leaned back in his seat. 'However, you are in possession of something much more valuable. My child, my blood, my future.'

A shiver of awareness prickled over Emma's skin, the words resonating inside her. Sober. Portentous. There was no escaping how real this was—and how deep in she was.

'You seem to forget that I came here of my own volition.' Swallowing the tightness in her throat, she fought to stand her ground. 'I chose to tell you about the baby, when I could easily have kept quiet about the whole thing.'

'And you expect me to be grateful for that?' His words were chilling.

'No, not grateful exactly.' She looked down. 'But I didn't expect to be treated with such suspicion.'

'You have already betrayed my trust once, Emma. Therefore, I will treat you accordingly.'

Emma bit down hard on her lip. Leo had the infuriating capacity to twist her in knots every way she turned. 'I explained about that.'

His dismissive shrug said it all. But seemingly bored with tormenting her, he rose to pour himself another drink. Turning back, he trained his level gaze on her face.

'I have given some thought to the situation and come to a conclusion.'

Had he, now? But something about his fixed stare silenced Emma's rebellion.

'I have decided that we will get married.'

Leo watched Emma's mouth fall open in astonishment, not without some gratification. 'Married?'

'*Sì,* straight away. There is nothing to be gained by waiting.' He pushed on, watching her reaction intently. It felt good to be in control again.

Panic joined her astonishment. 'No... I mean...we can't.'

'We can and we will.'

Her hands separated a length of hair, pulling it over one shoulder, twisting it round and around. 'I think you must still be in shock, Leo.'

Ha! The only one in shock was her. 'I can assure you I am perfectly rational.' He offered her a raised brow of sincerity. 'Marriage is the only solution.'

Her mouth twitched, then pursed. He could almost see her mind whirring as she formed her next objection.

'Why would you consider such a drastic step before the baby is even born?'

Leo hesitated. 'Because no child of mine will be born out of wedlock.' Despite his caution, the growled words rose from somewhere deep inside him. From a dark place where the wounds of his own illegitimacy still lingered. Still festered. And Emma had noticed. There was a quizzical look in those blue eyes. Leo reined himself back in.

'But this is the twenty-first century.' She continued to watch him closely. 'Nobody worries about a child being born out of wedlock these days.'

'*I* do.' Still too vehement, he could see Emma trying to figure him out, to get inside his head. Well that wasn't going to happen. 'Practical decisions need to be made. It is vitally important to have everything on a legal footing from the start. I have seen too many deals go wrong through lack of forward planning.'

'But this isn't a business deal, Leo.' Her soft mouth pouted. 'This is a baby!'

'All the more reason then.' He shot her a punishing stare, designed to silence her objections, to quash the curiosity in her eyes. And when that didn't work, he took a firmer stance. 'We are getting married, Emma, and that's an end to it.'

Emma watched as Leo picked up his briefcase, clicking it open to remove a sheaf of papers. For one crazy minute she thought it was a marriage licence, that Leo had somehow contrived to forgo any sort of ceremony and have her bound to him with nothing more than a signature. But it was a different contract he had in his hand. A pre-nup.

'I have had the details drawn up. It is all quite straightforward, but if you want my lawyers to go over anything with you, it can be arranged.'

'I have no interest in your vast fortune, Leo.' Emma tried for a scornful huff but beneath the derision lay hollow despondency. How could he know her so little as to think she would care about his money?

'*Bene*. Then there should be no problem.' He closed the space between them with a couple of strides, the papers in his hand, coming to sit beside her. So close she could feel the warmth from his thigh setting her senses alight, making it hard to breathe. 'I will leave these for you to read through. My lawyer will be here to witness our signatures in the morning.'

This was the way Leo operated. Ordered, fast paced, everything done to his precise instructions. Work, leisure, lovers. Only this afternoon Emma had brought chaos to his door. Now that chaos had been controlled, dealt with. She and the baby were just another business contract to be signed and sealed in the fastest possible time. A deal to be sewn up.

'I suggest the wedding takes place next week. Shall we say Tuesday?'

Very deliberately, he directed the full, lethal force of his gaze on her. As if he could impose his will through the power of his eyes alone. Maybe he could. Emma could think of a hundred reasons not to marry this man. A thousand. And yet…

Her heart gave a feeble stutter as she took in the hard perfection of his face, the strong, clean lines drawn tight, the granite set of his jaw. Despite the studied calm, she could sense the pressure he was under, see it in his eyes. The need to get this problem sorted. To fix it. Now. They were both fire-fighting the same blaze—just from different angles.

Duty, propriety and a fierce need to take control lay behind Leo's decision to marry. But first he had to future-proof himself against this woman who had the potential to wreck his life even more than she already had. Hence the pre-nup.

Whereas for Emma it was about protecting herself, her heart, her very sanity. She knew how badly this could end. Not because of any financial repercussions—his billions were quite safe. But because there was no escaping the way he made her feel. Somewhere deep down, somewhere she had no control over. Stirring up wild, reckless emotions that could only bring trouble. That could so easily tear her apart. The same emotions that had got her into this mess. There was no lawyer in the land that could draw up a contract to protect her from that.

'I don't remember agreeing to marry you at all, let alone on which day of the week.' She tilted her chin in rebellion, but turmoil swirled inside. Defiance was the only protection she had against this formidable man.

'But you will.' A command wrapped in silk. That cast-iron assurance that he could make her do whatever he wanted. That his will would be obeyed.

'Well, just supposing I did agree...' Emma felt like she was slowly slipping underwater, with nothing and no one to save her. 'What sort of marriage would it be? Just a legal document, or would you expect us to be a couple in...in the true sense of the word?'

She regretted her line of questioning before the words had even left her mouth. For Leo had gone frighteningly still, his dark stare, when Emma finally forced herself to find it, holding all the dangers she was trying so hard to avoid.

'That depends.' The thick swathe of his lashes lowered drowsily, but there was nothing sleepy about the challenge in his narrowed gaze.

'On what?' She rasped the question from a throat that was bone dry.

'On how we get on.' He lifted her hand from where it lay clenched in her lap, slowly unfurling her fingers one by one until they were both left staring at her open palm as if it could tell the future.

Emma snatched back her hand before every suppressed desire that Leo had to be deliberately stoking broke cover and betrayed her. The idea of permanently tying herself to Leo made her feel cut adrift from a reality that had already been dangerously shaky. Her stomach was twisting in all sorts of ways she couldn't begin to address. A complicated mix of emotions too tightly knotted to unpick. But she had to be practical now. She had to try and think with her head.

Agreeing to marry Leo *did* make sense, so was there any point in making a battle out of it? For one, she would never win. Leo Ravenino was a skilled negotiator, a ruthless businessman, someone who always got what he wanted in both his public and personal life. She had no chance against such a man.

But, more important, what would she be battling against? As she stared into Leo's flint-grey eyes, fighting with everything she had to ward off their hypnotic spell, she had to admit that the security he was offering was tempting.

Emma was used to fighting her own battles. She felt like she'd been doing it her whole life. She had been telling the truth when she'd informed Leo she would be prepared to raise their child alone. But that didn't mean she wasn't scared. She would love it with all her heart, she had no doubt about that, but was love enough?

It wasn't like she could go to her mother for guidance. Their views on parenting were polar opposites—Emma had no intention of subjecting her child to the sort of upbringing she had had. Far from being someone to turn to, her troubled relationship with her mother only added to her worries. What if there was something wrong in her genetic make-up, meaning that the child failed to bond with her, the way she had failed to bond with her own mother? Or that she passed on the insecurities that had so disturbed her own childhood, that still lurked dark and silent in her soul. The responsibility of raising a child was immense. Supposing she wasn't up to it?

And even if these fears were unfounded, there was the financial situation. Since losing

her job she hadn't been able to find any work
with real security, just picking up whatever
she could to keep the money coming in. The
gig economy may have kept the wolf from
the door, but it was still there, crouching on
the garden path, ready to pounce at any moment. She lived in a dingy room in a shared
house, she had no help and very little money.
Whichever way you looked at it, it wasn't a
great way to welcome a baby into this world.

Then there was the other big one. Emma
believed every child deserved two parents.
Despite her mother refusing to ever discuss
her father, let alone allowing her to try and
contact him, it still hadn't stopped a young
Emma from fantasising about finding him
one day, establishing a relationship with him,
maybe even going to live with him. A fantasy
she had still nurtured as she had hurriedly
packed her bags to leave home that fateful
day. Only to have her mother cruelly dash her
dreams. *'And don't go thinking you can run
back to your daddy, because you can't. He's
dead.'* Emma could still remember the look
of triumph on her mother's face.

The wave of grief for the man she had never
known had hit her hard, her sorrow far deeper
and more painful than logic demanded. After
all, he had abandoned her. Struggling to pro-

cess the rest of her mother's gloating rage, she just about managed to glean a few details, that he had been killed in a riding accident two years previously. That the world was better off without him.

Her regret at never knowing her father still ran dark and deep. Given the choice, she knew she would never want to subject her own child to such a fate. And Leo was giving her that choice. He may have wreaked havoc in her life, turned it upside down and shaken it so hard she barely knew which way was up, but he was facing up to his responsibilities. He would always be there for their child; Emma had no doubt about that. He could give them both the security that had been painfully lacking in her own childhood. Be the second parent she so wanted their son or daughter to have. He was offering to marry her—no, not offering, insisting. But who was she to challenge that? Deep down, she, too, would like their child to be born in wedlock, in a way that neither she nor any of her siblings had been.

But the payoff for this security would be surrendering her independence, at least in the short term. Emma was under no illusions about that. Leo would expect them to live where he dictated they live, lead the life that he decided they would lead. No doubt it would be a life more comfortable, more extravagant than anything she had ever imagined. But Emma had never craved wealth. She did, however, have to accept that wealth brought opportunities. Maybe in time, when things had calmed down, she could use those opportunities to her advantage. Pick up her career again or go back to studying. Somehow she would find her independence again, she just needed to be clever about it.

Far more worrying was the way Leo affected her, deep down. Could she marry a man who squeezed her skin tight over her bones with nothing more than a glance from those grey eyes? Whose hard-edged words and ruthless determination left her feeling hollowed out, empty, as if she had lost something she hadn't even known she'd had?

Leo Ravenino was the epitome of the alpha male. A powerful, hugely successful man at the top of his game. A man who made all the decisions, called all the shots. Power was in his genes, in the set of his shoulders, the length of his stride. It was the blood in his veins, hardwired in his brain. It made him who he was. To try and fight this control would be futile, like attempting to hold back the tide.

But for all his high-handed autocracy Emma was forced to admit that Leo's proposition was an honourable one. Should she just accept it? Did she have any choice?

'So, are we in agreement?' Leo broke the silence, his hands resting in his lap, his eyes never leaving her face, as if he had been tracking her thoughts. 'The wedding will go ahead on Tuesday?'

'Very well.' Emma took in the biggest, bravest breath of her life. 'I agree. It will.'

CHAPTER SEVEN

MORE DEEP BREATHS were needed today.

Morning had dawned clear and bright, like every other morning since Emma had been here at Villa Magenta. Outside, the parkland sparkled in the low sunshine, long shadows dramatically striping the grass, holding on to the dew, as the birds hopped around looking for their breakfast.

But the shutters to Emma's room were firmly closed. Her bed was empty, there was no sign of life. Until you went into the bathroom...

Pushing herself back on her heels, her fingers still gripping the cold porcelain of the toilet bowl, Emma felt her stomach churn again. Morning sickness. This was horrible. She concentrated on taking some restorative breaths, wondering how long it was going to last. Wondering why it had had to kick in today of all days—the day of her wedding.

Didn't she have enough to cope with already?

Mercifully, the ceremony was going to be very low key. Informing her that he had booked a register office in Milan for eleven thirty on the morning of the seventh, just five days after Emma had arrived in Milan, Leo had brusquely enquired whether she wanted any of her family to attend, and gave a nod of approval when she had declined.

Presumably he wanted to get this over with with the minimum of fuss as much as she did. Emma had never been one to fantasise about having a big white wedding, never given it much thought. But now she wondered what it would be like to be marrying through choice, not circumstance, to be embarking upon a loving relationship with someone you looked forward to spending the rest of your life with. To feel the swell of love in your heart, instead of this dull, hollow ache.

But she had to face facts. This was a marriage of convenience, even if nothing about it felt remotely convenient right now. She was tying herself to a ruthless businessman purely to secure the future of their unborn child. Marrying a man who, had she not been pregnant, she would never have seen again. And as for embarking on a loving relationship, looking forward to spending the rest of their lives together, neither of those things was remotely feasible. This was simply a practical solution to a difficult problem. A means to an end, a sensible, pragmatic approach to… Oh, God… Emma hung her head over the toilet bowl. She was going to be sick again…

The register office loomed into view, Leo parking his red sports car in one of the allotted bays with typical Latin flair. Coming around to open the door for her, Emma carefully stepped out, fighting to control her breathing, the thud of her heart…*the instinct to pick up her skirt and run as fast as she could in the opposite direction.*

Smoothing her hands over her dress, she concentrated on arranging it just so, the cream silk fabric suddenly completely absorbing, anything to distract herself from what she was about to do. Chosen from a selection that had mysteriously appeared the day before for her perusal, the style was a simple sleeveless shift, no frills or flounces but beautifully cut so that it fitted her perfectly. All that was left was to paste on what she hoped passed for a semblance of a smile. At least she had stopped feeling sick.

The ceremony was over in a matter of minutes. Stepping out into the bright sunshine, Emma no longer bore the name Quinn, the surname of a man she had never known, but Ravenino, the surname of a man she barely knew. There was an irony there, if Emma had the capacity to dwell on it. Which she didn't, because she was way too busy trying to control the jumping nerves, the surge of adrenaline threatening to take her legs from under her.

For a moment they stood silently facing each other, caught in the enormity of what they had just done. Shading her eyes, Emma tipped back her head to look at the man who was now her husband. Standing tall and proud, immaculately dressed in a dark suit and a grey tie, he was every woman's fantasy of the perfect groom. Hot, hard male perfection. But with his eyes hidden behind designer sunglasses, she wasn't able to read his expression, only his unnatural stillness betraying any sense of unease.

She realised she had no idea what he was thinking, what life held in store for her and her unborn child. Twisting the new gold ring on her finger, she found herself wondering, yet again, just how she was going to cope with a life so changed, with a man she knew so little of yet who still managed to affect her so deeply.

'I should get back to the office.' Leo's attention was drawn to his car, where a couple of teenaged boys were peering inside enviously. 'Do you have any plans for the afternoon?'

'No, not really.' Emma swallowed. What plans would she have, other than trying to figure out how she was going to live the rest of her life?

'Well, you have a car at your disposal.' Leo indicated the sleek black limo that Emma now saw had pulled up alongside the kerb. 'Luigi will take you anywhere you want to go.'

'And has he been instructed to make sure I don't escape, like before?' She raised her chin.

'No.' His lethal focus was back on her, steel in his voice. Emma blinked, her startled face reflected in the lenses of his glasses. 'We are married now, legally bound, the documents all signed. I no longer need to keep track of you. Should there be any transgressions, it would be a matter for the lawyers.'

Well, that made her feel *so* much better. 'There won't be any transgressions,' Emma huffed quickly. 'Not on my part at least.'

She hoped she sounded authoritative but,

truth be told, she had no idea what she'd signed. When the lawyer had arrived to witness their signatures on the pre-nup, she had almost snatched the pen out of his hand in her hurry to sign her name at the bottom of the pages. Done to show Leo that she had zero interest in his billions, her hurry had also stopped her from thinking too deeply about what she was doing. Which had been pretty much the only way to stop her hand from shaking.

'Neither will there be any transgressions on my part.' Raising his sunglasses, Leo pushed them up onto his head, ruffling his hair in a way that made Emma want to reach out, delve her fingers through the silky dark waves, feel them brush against the sensitive skin of her palms.

'Well, that's good.' She lowered her eyes to try and escape the persistent, unwanted tug of desire. 'I'm glad we've got that sorted.'

'*Sì.*' There was a second's silence before Emma felt the stroke of a finger against her cheek, so light as to almost not be there but enough to draw her gaze upwards, to set her senses on fire.

'I hope you don't find the prospect of being married to me too alarming, Emma.' His finger traced down to her chin, his eyes solemn, questioning.

'No.' With the trail of his touch doing terrible things to her insides she hotly denied everything she felt. 'Why would I?'

'Why indeed?' The words were softly spoken, his eyes darkening.

Emma stayed very still. Alarm was only one of many emotions Leo could stir so easily in her. The mere touch of his finger was triggering the slow stealth of pleasure. A part of her wanted Leo to lean in and kiss her so badly her whole body ached for it. Another part wanted to bury herself in a deep black hole to protect her from all the ways he could make her feel. Did he know the effect he had on her? It was impossible to tell.

She pulled in a breath to calm her nerves. Whatever else, she had to try and keep her wayward feelings to herself. To let Leo see how he affected her, deep down in that intensely private place, would only give him more power. Strengthen a hold on her that was already far too tight.

'I'm fine.' She moved a step away to release herself from the torture of his touch. Her voice sounded hollow, even to her own ears. 'You don't need to worry about me.'

'*Bene.*' Replacing his sunglasses, Leo returned to the brisk businesslike persona that Emma felt far more comfortable with. '*A proposito*, I have booked a table for tonight. I thought we should do something to mark the occasion of our marriage. I trust you are okay with that?'

'Yes, of course.' Emma nodded with far more enthusiasm than she felt. 'That would be nice.'

Nice? She screwed up her face. It was hardly a ringing endorsement and judging by the way Leo's mouth had tightened, he'd noticed it too. But, then, he noticed everything.

'In the meantime, I suggest you go shopping for something to wear. Whatever you want. Luigi will drive you.'

Emma hesitated. Shopping wasn't really her thing, but on the other hand she had brought so few clothes with her she badly needed a new wardrobe. Maybe if she bought a few practical outfits, and something posher for occasions like this dinner, which she was already dreading, that would be a sensible idea. Of course, it wouldn't be long before she'd be needing maternity clothes, but Emma decided she'd cross that bridge when she came to it. There was only so much upheaval a girl could take at one time.

'Thank you.' She politely accepted Leo's offer. 'I'll do that.'

'*Prego.*' Stepping closer, Leo brushed her cheek with his lips, just once, just enough to send her senses reeling again. 'I will see you later.'

Emma stared in amazement at the items that had been delivered to the villa. Had she really bought all this? Spread out in her dressing room, the sleek carrier bags bearing famous names that Emma had only read about in magazines stared defiantly back at her. Boxes tied with satin ribbons invited her to step closer for a better look.

No, this was ridiculous. She had gone mad. She would send them back. But as she lifted the first dress from its scented tissue paper, holding it against her body, she was seduced all over again. The cobalt blue fabric was so beautiful, the cut of the dress so clever, holding her in in all the right places. Buying the matching shoes and bag had seemed eminently sensible at the time. As had purchasing those perfectly fitting jeans in four different colours, not to mention the silk shirts, the soft leather jacket, the floaty summer skirt. And the lingerie... Slowly lifting the lid on one of the pale pink boxes, Emma broke the seal on the black tissue paper, her heart beating faster as she withdrew the bra and matching panties. They were so stunning they were like a work of art. She ran her fingers over the sheer fabric, imagining wearing them, imagining Leo looking at her wearing them… Enough! Hastily replacing them in the box, she slammed the lid back down. Whatever was she thinking?

But the shopping trip had been Leo's idea, not hers. Maybe she needed to consider what *he* had been thinking. Was he trying to turn her into one of the women he normally dated? Sophisticated, refined. It was a depressing thought. Because Emma was neither of those things and never would be. She now bore the name Ravenino and lived in a stunning home fit for a princess. She would wear these beautiful clothes if that was what her husband wanted. But inside she was still Emma Quinn—still trying to find her place in the world.

Walking over to the window, Emma gazed out at the lush rolling green parkland. All her life she had felt like the outsider, even within her own family. Much as she loved her younger siblings, they were a very different breed. A tightly knit pack, they appeared unfazed by the fact they had different fathers, embracing the chaos of their lifestyle with a carefree enthusiasm solemn Emma had never felt, not even when she was a child. They were also adored by their mother. Something Emma had never been.

Leaving home, she had concentrated all her efforts on her journalism career, securing the job on the *Paladin* her proudest achievement, even if it had been short-lived. But if she was being totally honest, she had never really fitted in there either. Certainly not with the old-timers and their extended lunches and waistlines to match, or even the bright young things, discussing their social lives at high volume, meeting for drinks after work.

Now she had a new life to get her head around, a new role as wife and mother. Truth be told, she felt woefully ill-equipped for either, but that didn't mean she couldn't do it. With a surge of optimism Emma squinted against the evening horizon. Fancy clothes might not turn her into a Hollywood star, but she was strong and she was brave. And she had integrity. Her commitment to Leo might have been squeezed out of her, more coercion than seduction, but now she was married she was determined to make the best of it.

Not that it had got off to a very promising start… Since being at Villa Magenta, Leo had treated her with a polite but cool reserve. All traces of the man who had made her blush that first evening about the way their marriage might play out banished behind a granite façade. That was when she actually saw him at all. Spending his days in his office in Milan, when he finally returned to the villa their exchanges were brief, their evening meals taken separately.

And as for their bedrooms… Villa Magenta was huge and Emma's quarters were situated way across the other side of the building from Leo's. Almost like it had been done deliberately. If Emma had nurtured any foolish hope that this week she and Leo would start to get to know one another, maybe settle her nerves and silence some of the nagging doubts, it had been severely dashed. Leo clearly had no interest in any such thing. Standing in front of the officiant that morning, the tall, dark Italian beside her had been as much a stranger as ever. The enormity of what she was about to do more bewildering than ever.

But the deed was done. They were now married, legally man and wife, and Emma was going to hang on to her optimism and make this work. After all, tonight was their wedding night and, despite everything, she couldn't hold back a feral sort of thrill. Despite the aching uncertainty, her imagination kept leaping ahead, her memory rushing to recall the one night they had shared, where every erotic detail was meticulously stored.

Seeing Leo again, being in his presence, had brought it all vividly back to life. The sound of his voice, the way he shrugged his shoulders, narrowed his eyes, used his hands to express himself all setting her pulse racing, her muscles clenching in memory. So far she had done her very best to hide her reaction from him. Maybe tonight she could stop pretending.

Heading towards the bathroom, Emma stripped off her clothes and stepped under the shower, the pounding hot water starting to ease the tension gripping her neck and shoulders. Reaching for the shower gel, she began to rhythmically soap her body, closing her eyes to inhale the delicious scent. Slowly, insidiously, a shudder of desire started to creep over her, stealthily making its way to her core. Snapping open her eyes, she turned off the water and wrapped herself in a white towel.

She didn't know what this evening would bring. She had no idea what was going on inside her husband's closed, calculating mind. But maybe she would wear that gorgeous underwear after all. Twisting a towel around her hair, she rubbed at the condensation on the mirror to find her wide-eyed reflection. Surely there could be no harm in that?

Leo watched through narrowed eyes as his wife made her way towards him. *His wife.* Words he had never thought he would use since leaving Ravenino. A situation he had never imagined finding himself in. His hands, held in his lap, flexed.

She looked different. Stunning, in fact. But the smile on her face was faint as she followed the maître d', the admiring glances of the male diners going unnoticed. Not by Leo, though. With a surge of possessiveness he rose, greeting her firmly with an outstretched arm, kissing her on both cheeks. She pulled away quickly.

'*Buonasera.*' He collected himself, drawing back her chair for her, signalling to the maître d' with a curt nod that his job was done.

'*Buonasera.*' She sat down. 'Not late, am I?'

She wasn't late. Unlike some of his previous dates, who seemed to think it added to their allure to arrive 'fashionably late', when all it did was irritate the hell out of him. From their brief acquaintance, he was relieved to find there were several things he liked about

Emma. She had an inner strength that he respected. No tantrums, no dramas. A level of detachment in the way she held her head high, tipped her chin that might even be called a challenge. Which was an interesting prospect. It had to be said: despite the turbulence of the last few days, she had conducted herself with the utmost decorum.

But right now decorum was the last thing on his mind—far from it. He allowed himself another glance as she opened her napkin, placing it on her lap, his eyes drawn to the creamy skin of her upper chest, the finely shaped collar bones. Unadorned. There was beauty enough as it was, but Leo found himself wondering what necklace he might buy for her, already imagining sweeping her hair to one side to fasten the clasp, lowering his head to plant a kiss on her skin.

This past week had been a lesson in self-control for him. A test to see how he felt about the startling new future he had embarked upon, to give himself time to figure out ways he was going to deal with it. And first on the list had been no sex. Keeping his distance would give him the chance to work things through in his head. Being seduced by her wide eyes and soft curves would not.

But tonight he found his resolve being severely tested.

In a gesture more hesitant than flirtatious, Emma touched her hair, which fell loose over her shoulders, meeting his gaze from beneath that fringe. Free from make-up, apart from a slash of red on her lips, she looked incredibly sexy.

Leo took a breath, reaching for his glass of water. No, he didn't want decorum tonight. He wanted wild, unfettered, hot, passionate, *dirty* sex. And he wanted it with the woman chewing her lip in front of him now. *Whoa.* He hurriedly took a sip of water then braced himself to face her again, feigning nonchalance. '*Sei molto carina*, you look lovely, by the way.'

'Thank you.' She gave an embarrassed laugh, a blush creeping up her neck, staining her cheeks until she had to reach for the menu to fan herself. 'Sorry.' She offered a rueful smile. 'It's the hormones, I expect.'

Was it? Or did she just not know how to accept a compliment? Did she really not realise how beautiful she was?

'The same hormones that made you so ill this morning?' Leo felt for safer ground.

Emma shot him a look as she laid down the menu. 'You know about that?'

'Yes.' He returned her stare. 'Maria told me you only wanted dry crackers for breakfast.'

'Is this how it's going to be?' Her shoulders stiffened. 'Are all my meals going to be policed by you?'

'I need to be aware if there are any problems.'

'It's not a problem, Leo, at least not for you. Morning sickness is perfectly normal at this stage of the pregnancy.'

Leo shrugged. He already knew that. In the short time since he had found out he was to be a father he had made it his business to learn everything he could about the various stages of pregnancy. Not that he had told Emma that.

'Are you hungry now?'

'Yes.' She seemed surprised at herself. 'I am.'

'*Bene*. Do you want me to translate the menu for you?'

'Yes, please.' Her shoulders dropped a little at last. 'In fact…' she peered at him from around the menu '…perhaps you should choose for me, as you know this restaurant, I mean.'

'*Certo.*' Leo suppressed a small smile at her solemn expression. 'As long as I'm not going to be accused of policing what you eat?'

'You have my permission.' She matched his teasing tone. 'This time.'

Emma ate her meal enthusiastically, which Leo noted with pleasure. She denied wanting a dessert, but he ordered her one anyway, watching with satisfaction as she spooned creamy gelato into her mouth, polished off the last biscotti.

They kept the conversation light, polite, both of them feeling their way, being careful not to trample on the new shoots of their relationship. But Emma had the sort of face that spelled out her emotions even when she didn't want it to, and more than once Leo caught a glimpse of wariness behind the composed façade.

'How's your water?' He posed the question lightly.

Emma laughed. 'Good. I can definitely taste the slopes of Mount Fuji.'

She had stuck to water all evening, her face a picture when the sommelier had presented her with a menu to choose from. Picking one at random, she had waited until his back was turned before self-consciously informing Leo that the water she normally drank came out of a tap.

He sat back in his chair, waiting for Emma to pick up the conversation again, watching her from beneath weighted eyelids. The hum in his blood had not left him all evening, the dark need to take his wife to his bed pressing down on him more forcefully than ever. But he would not give in to it. Yet.

He straightened his spine, resting his elbows on the table. He knew so little of the woman before him with the flushed cheeks and bright eyes. In his hurry to take control of the present he had scarcely given a thought to her past, her background. Now he found he wanted to know more. He wanted to know everything.

'Tell me about your family.' He steepled his fingers, resting his chin on the tips.

Emma's head came up, the flash in her eyes betraying her unease. 'There's not much to tell really.'

Instinctively Leo knew that wasn't true. He let his silence speak for him.

'It's just my mum and my siblings. My father left when I was a baby. I never knew him.'

Well, that made two of them.

'Siblings?'

'I'm the oldest of five. But we have different fathers.'

Interesting.

'And where do they live?'

'At the moment Somerset. But they move around, living in various communes in the south-west of England.'

'An unusual lifestyle?'

'Yes, well, alternative is the word my mother would use.' Her eyebrows went up. 'As a child I never went to school, never had a haircut, never wore shoes in the summer. It's the same for my brothers and sisters.'

'But you turned your back on that way of life?'

'Yes.' She traced a biscotti crumb around the tablecloth with her finger. 'Somehow I didn't really fit in. I was always the one begging to be sent to school. Can you believe that!' She pulled a face. 'I used to go to the library and read masses of books about children that went to boarding school and wore uniforms and played hockey, wishing I could be one of them. Stupid!'

No, it wasn't stupid. Leo's brief glimpse of the lonely child touched something inside.

'And your relationship with your family now?'

'I love my siblings, obviously. And my mother too. But our relationship has always been…complicated.'

'Why so?' Leo kept his voice deliberately neutral.

'A number of things.' Her sigh was short and sharp. 'I think she has always held me responsible for my father abandoning us.'

'But didn't you say you were just a baby?'

'Yes. But I was sickly and needy and screamed all the time. My father decided he'd had enough, leaving my mother to cope on her own. She was young, only nineteen.'

'But hardly fair to take it out on you?'

'Well, you can't help how you feel, I guess.' She tried for an accepting smile. 'And then later on there was something else…an unfortunate incident.' She stopped, pursing her lips together as if to physically prevent herself from saying any more. But there was no way Leo was going to let it rest there.

'What kind of incident?'

'It doesn't matter.'

'What kind of incident, Emma?' Leo heard the growl in his voice.

'Just a man my mother was seeing.' She lowered her eyes. 'He came on to me…and when I told my mother…well, let's just say she didn't take my side.'

Leo went very still, the primal, protective instinct inside him poised, ready to pounce. Emma's tone was even, clipped into neat sentences, but it was obvious how much this had affected her.

'When you say "came on" to you…' His hands curled into fists. 'What exactly do you mean?'

'It was my sixteenth birthday.' Another sigh, as if she was trying to make out it was all rather boring. *Like hell it was.* 'There was a party, the usual sort of gathering, people singing and dancing and drinking too much. Smoking weed. Not me, of course, I've never been into any of that. But this guy… my mum's boyfriend, he…he said he'd got a present for me, that I was to follow him. He led me into this copse, pushed me down and then…he threw himself on top of me.'

'*Cristo*, Emma!'

'It's okay.' She rushed to reassure him. 'I managed to get away. Luckily, he was really drunk, so I managed to wriggle out from under him.'

Leo felt his blood pressure soar. This scumbag needed to be tracked down and castrated.

'But when I told Mum, she didn't believe me. She said I must have led him on. That he had turned me down and now I was trying to make trouble.' Emma chewed the corner of her lip. 'So, the next day, when the guy left, she blamed me for that too. She said it was just like with my father…that I was a curse on her relationships...that I couldn't bear to see her happy. But it really wasn't like that.'

Her touching need to make him see she had done nothing wrong punched right through him. She didn't need to prove herself to him. Not in this instance. 'I was just trying to protect her, make her see the sort of man he really was.'

Dio santo. Leo had to take a moment to calm himself down. He already loathed this woman who had treated Emma so despicably. Instead of supporting her daughter, a vulnerable young woman who had just suffered a serious assault, she had turned against her, accusing her. What kind of mother did that? And as for that creature that called himself a man...

Instinctively he felt for Emma's hand, clasping it tightly in his. Too tightly, as Emma's wide-eyed surprise made clear. He forced himself to let go, to sit back, take a breath. But one thing was for sure. From now on, anyone who tried to hurt his wife would have him to answer to.

'And that was when you moved to London?' He needed to concentrate on the facts.

'Yes. I couldn't stay...not after that. We both agreed it would be best to put some space between us. I had signed up to do A levels at the local college, but those plans had to change. Moving to London meant getting a job as soon as I could and continuing my education in my spare time.'

'And I'm guessing that wasn't easy at such a young age.'

'No, but I survived. I'm tougher than I look.' Her brave smile killed him. 'And it was actually quite empowering. A whole new life.'

A life that Leo had torn apart. A life that she had been carefully constructing for years, brought down around her ears. By him. No! Leo corrected himself. Emma had brought this on herself. She deserved to be punished for that article, even if she had submitted it in error. The fault lay with her, no matter how much that innocent gaze might try and say otherwise.

He raised his eyes, ready to challenge the guilt that refused to be banished. The guilt that she had to be deliberately provoking with her guileless air. But, try as he might, he could see no sign of it in the glitter of her eyes. Instead he saw something infinitely more troubling. Along with her stoic acceptance, Leo realised that she was putting her faith in him to make things right. Not practically, he would have no problem with that.

But emotionally. And that was what clawed at his throat. Because by looking for the good in him, she was searching for a man he could never be.

Leo tore his eyes away from her face. Suddenly the restaurant felt far too hot, stifling, oppressive, the other diners too loud, their chatter a cacophony of meaningless noise. He tugged at his tie, undoing the top button of his shirt to run two fingers around the inside of his collar.

Suddenly Emma's acceptance felt like deceit. Her faith like some sort of trickery to get inside his head. Why would she so easily forgive a man who had lost her her job, stolen her virginity, made her pregnant after one night of selfish indulgence? He had been taken in by her guile once, it wasn't going to happen again. Right now he needed answers.

'Why were you still a virgin the night we met?' The question shot from his mouth, harsh, interrogatory, as if *she* was the one who had done something wrong.

Emma gave him a defensive look, heavy lashes blinking rapidly. 'I don't know, I just was.'

'Not good enough, Emma.' The guilt inside him had sharpened like a blade and he would use it as a weapon. 'Why would someone who had never had sex before choose to do so with a man they had only just met?' *A man like me.* The words stayed silent in his head, but they were there, pressing down on him. *A cold, callous, son-of-a-bitch who took what he wanted and to hell with anyone else.*

'The simple answer is that I'd never met anyone I wanted to have sex with before.' Her frankness did nothing to ease his guilt. Far from gloating, it only increased his shame.

'And the complicated one?'

'Well, I guess if a psychiatrist got into my head, they might say I had "issues" about sexual relationships.' She gave another nervous laugh, twisting a strand of hair around her finger in that way she did. 'I was never comfortable with the whole "free love" thing that my mother subscribed to, different partners coming and going all the time. And then when that guy…did what he did…'

'He assaulted you, Emma. Why can't you just say it?'

'Okay, when that guy…' she took a breath '…*assaulted* me…it just turned me off the whole idea of sex at all. So I sort of closed myself down.'

Her softly flushed face stared back at him, open, innocent, torturing Leo still further.

'So I guess I should thank you.' A tentative smile lit her eyes.

'Thank me?' The growl in his voice was meant as a warning.

'Yes.' A warning she seemed determined to ignore. 'Because you made me realise I wasn't the hollow shell of a woman I was starting to think I was. That the issues I had weren't insurmountable. You made me feel for the first time, Leo. Really feel.'

Her hand fluttered down onto the table. For one awful moment Leo thought she was going to reach for his, take his balled fist and try and smooth it out for comfort or support when he could give her neither. But instead her fingers felt for the edge of her napkin, smoothing over the linen.

A storm of conflicting emotions roared in Leo's head. He had to get away. Right now. Put some space between him and the bright blue eyes that were so innocently holding him to account. The softly seductive curves that were still determined to torment his body. But he would not give in to his desires. No way. Denial would be his penance—even if it was too little too late.

'We should leave.' Scraping back his chair, he moved behind Emma's so she would be in no doubt that this was a command, not a suggestion.

'Of course.' He heard the surprise in her voice, but she immediately gathered herself, standing up, flicking her hair over one shoulder. Leo caught the scent of it, soft and floral, assaulting his senses. His eyes strayed to the pale skin of her neck left exposed. He swallowed hard, fighting the urge to lean forward and press his lips against that delicate flesh, to heat it with his breath, trail his mouth upwards. Lights flashed behind his momentarily closed lids.

She turned, so close now she had to be able to feel the heat emanating from him, sense the ache in his groin that refused to lessen. With a monumental effort he took a step back, his resolve tested beyond all limits when he caught the raw emotion glittering in her eyes.

Taking her arm, Leo hurried them between the tables of diners, heads turning in surprise at their rapid departure. Finally in the car, his hands gripped the steering wheel as he impatiently waited for Emma to put on her seat belt. With a roar of the engine he pulled the car out onto the road, grateful for Emma's silence. For the darkness all around him muffling his punishing thoughts.

CHAPTER EIGHT

'A GOOD STRONG HEARTBEAT.' The sonographer steadied the transducer over Emma's gel-covered abdomen. 'Can you hear that?'

Emma nodded, not trusting herself to speak. She *could* hear it—that remarkable pulsing, whooshing sound of a new life growing inside her. Standing close beside her, Leo had gone completely silent, not even appearing to breathe.

'You can make out the arms and legs quite clearly.' The transducer moved around. 'And here…this is the baby's spine.'

Emma stared at the blurry black and white image on the screen, emotion choking her throat. This was the most amazing thing she had ever seen.

'I'm just going to take a few measurements now, and then I'll be able to give you a predicted due date.'

Beside her, she felt Leo shift, clearing his

throat before addressing the sonographer in Italian.

'*Non ci sono problemi? E tutto normale?*'

'*Sì, tutto normale.* Perfectly normal.'

The sonographer turned to smile at them both, before looking back at the screen. For a moment all went quiet as she clicked and dragged dotted lines over the images, concentrating on making her calculations, before finally pronouncing, 'February the fourteenth!' She beamed at them. 'A Valentine baby!'

A Valentine baby. Biting down on her lip to stop the wobble, Emma forced herself to smile back. This baby hardly epitomised love and romance, hearts and flowers. Far from it. Wild, uncontrollable passion in the moment, that couldn't be denied. But since then nothing but formal exchanges, polite, clipped conversations. It seemed to Emma that Leo was deliberately going out of his way to flatten their relationship. To douse the glimmer of any flame before it had a chance to catch hold.

But here was their baby, already so perfect, its tiny heart beating inside her, quietly preparing itself for its entrance to the world. And even though it had thrown her own world into chaos, forcing her to rush into a marriage with a man she couldn't begin to know, who refused to give anything of himself yet still threatened to undo her with his every glance, Emma knew this baby was the most miraculous, incredible thing that had ever happened to her.

Accepting the proffered paper towel, she rubbed the gel off her tummy, then straightened her blouse and swung her legs over the examination table. The sonographer was printing off the images of the scan, about to hand them to Emma, when Leo reached forward to take them from her.

'*Grazie.*' He didn't examine them but, folding the strip carefully, tucked it into the pocket of his white linen shirt.

'We will book you in for a twenty-week scan,' the sonographer continued. 'By then I will be able to tell you the baby's sex. Should you wish to know, of course.'

Back out in the bright sunshine, heading down the bustling street towards where their car was parked, Emma waited for Leo to say something. Anything. But instead he stared resolutely ahead, his lips firmly closed, and Emma felt the swell of hurt rise to her throat. Was he really not going to make any comment on the amazing thing they had just seen? Almost like he was pretending it hadn't happened. Eventually she could stand it no longer. As they stood on the edge of the kerb, waiting for the lights to change so they could cross several busy lanes of traffic, she shaded her eyes to gaze at his profile.

'So, what did you think?' She kept her voice level, non-confrontational, even though his lack of emotion made her want to beat her fists against his granite chest. 'The scan was remarkable, wasn't it? The way you could see so much when the baby is still so tiny.'

'*Sì.*'

Emma waited. *Was that it? Was that really all he had to say?* But despite the growing ache, like he was pressing on a bruise, despite the imperious profile that refused to turn her way, Emma would not give up. Because giving up meant admitting defeat. Admitting that not only did Leo have no time for her but he had no time for their baby either. And that was more than she could bear.

'How big did she say it was?' She swallowed down her hurt, her pride. 'One and a half inches?'

'*Sì.*' He was staring hard enough at the traffic to make it stop by willpower alone. A bus slowed as it went past, and Emma saw the two of them reflected in its dark glass windows. Leo, stony faced but still effortlessly cool in casual chinos, standing almost a foot taller than Emma, whose hair was blowing around her shoulders. They looked mismatched. They looked like strangers.

When the lights finally changed Leo took her arm and hurried her through the throng of pedestrians. On the other side, Emma hastened her stride to match his, even though the intense heat was making her sweat. She pulled in a breath, digging deep to find her last reserves of resilience. Determination, stubbornness, a blind optimism that she could start to make Leo start to thaw driving her on.

'Shall we find out the sex of the baby at the next scan?' The speed of their steps was making her breathless. 'Or would you rather keep it as a surprise?'

'I don't know, Emma.' At last he stopped, turning to address her, but his words were cold, irritable. 'And frankly now is not the time to discuss it.'

Emma met his dark stare. 'Why not?'

'Because I have a pile of work waiting for me on my desk, two conference calls to make, and a trustees' meeting to chair. So, if you don't mind, perhaps we can leave this conversation for another time.'

They had reached the side road now where Leo's car was parked, its lights flashing as Leo clicked the key fob.

Emma looked away, defeated. She was so tired of pretending. To herself and to Leo. Tired of trying to make out that everything was okay when it wasn't. Tired of swallowing down the knot of hurt, only to have it unravel inside her, wrap itself around her internal organs and squeeze ever tighter. She was tired of being brave, constantly having to fight off rejection. Rejection that hurt more with every passing day.

These past few weeks had been exhausting. Physically and mentally draining, until Emma wasn't sure she had a drop of resilience left. She had started this journey not knowing what to expect of her marriage, but that hadn't stopped her from nurturing foolish hopes. Hopes that she and Leo might start to get to know and like each other, take pleasure in each other's company, not just as prospective parents but as man and wife. In every sense of the word.

Ha! Bitterness tore through her. At her own naivety, stupidity. Because those hopes had been cruelly crushed. Not least on her wedding night.

She still cringed when she thought back to the meal in the restaurant. All done up in her posh frock, trying to be positive about a future she had no control over, optimism cloaking common sense. She had put on fancy underwear, for God's sake. Paused in front of the mirror to admire what the clever cut did to her silhouette. How it made her feel sexy. She had imagined Leo looking at her, wanting her, the way she wanted him, despite everything. Taking her…

Now her cheeks just burned with humiliation. For Leo had not wanted her. Despite her best efforts to play the part of his new bride, she had got it all wrong. As had been clearly demonstrated during the silent ride home, the curt nod of goodnight as the doors of the villa had closed behind them. The sight of his broad back striding away from her.

Alone in her bedroom she had stripped naked, balling the offensive underwear to hurl it into the corner of the room, hot tears pricking the backs of her eyes.

But a new day had brought a new perspective. Giving herself a stern talking to, Emma had thrown back the curtains, determined to face facts as they were. In short, she had to get real. Leo had only married her because of the baby. There was no secret about that. But she had married him for the same reason. In that regard they were quits. She just had to keep her head straight, swallow down the humiliation of that night and focus on what was important. Their baby. The baby was all that mattered.

Which was why this latest rejection was such a slap in the face. Leo might not be interested in her, but his lack of interest in the baby hurt—really hurt. And like a mother lion Emma felt her protective instincts rising up, heating her blood. She opened her mouth to tell him just what she thought of him, then stopped. What was the point? It would be like attacking a lump of granite with a rubber hammer. Exposing nothing but her own deeply held insecurities.

Instead she turned on her heel, marching off in the opposite direction as fast as she could, her sandals snapping on the pavement, hair flying. If she put enough space between them, she might just be able to control the turmoil that was threatening to engulf her. The hurt that was threatening to crack her apart.

But Leo was beside her in a second, his hand on her arm, turning her to face him. His shadow fell across her, his face a tight mask of annoyance. 'Where do you think you are going?'

'Anywhere as long as it's away from you.' Emma forced the words through a choking throat.

A muscle spasmed in Leo's cheek, his famous control slipping very slightly. 'Explain yourself.'

Just that. Cold, imperious. Emma tried for a dismissive stare, tried to start walking again but Leo blocked her way, waiting.

'How about you work it out for yourself?' Her breath heaved in her chest.

'I will do no such thing.' A dark scowl marred his face. 'You are coming back to the car and I am taking you home.'

'No.' Emma stood firm, although the quake in her voice was getting harder and harder to control. 'I will find my own way back, thank you very much. And it's not my home, anyway. I don't have a home.'

'What are you talking about?' Leo's fierce gaze scorched over her face. 'Of course you have a home. Several homes, in fact.'

'They are not my homes, they're yours. Everything is yours—the cars, the houses, even the clothes I am wearing were bought by you.' Her words rushed out, trying to beat the tears she knew weren't far behind. 'All I have is a baby you don't want.'

The air between them stilled.

'Now you are being ridiculous.'

'Am I?' Her voice finally cracked and she stifled a sob. 'Or am I just spelling out the truth?'

'Look, Emma…' She could see the effort it was taking to try and be reasonable in the set of his jaw, the grit in his voice. His hands found her arms, lightly running over her skin, leaving it prickling beneath his touch. Reaching her wrists, he pressed his thumbs against her ragged pulse. 'I can only assume this unreasonable behaviour is due to your condition.'

Emma took in a breath of scorched air. Shaking his hands from her wrists, she was ready to fly at him, but a woman was coming along the narrow street behind them, walking a tiny dog on a lead.

'It has nothing to do with my condition.' She hissed the words through clenched teeth. The woman was alongside them now, looking at them curiously. Even the little dog seemed interested. Fighting to compose herself, Emma waited for them to pass. 'And everything to do with your arrogant, overbearing attitude.'

'Is that so?' Leo shoved his hands into his pockets, his casual pose fooling neither of them. 'You are very quick to point out my failings, Emma.'

'It's not difficult.' Her eyes blazed.

'Then I am only sorry that I am not the man you want me to be.'

'No, you're not sorry.' Her words came out in a rush of hurt and fury and sheer frustrated impotence. 'You couldn't care less. You intend to carry on with your life exactly as you always have—working and travelling and doing deals and, and…bedding beautiful women too, for all I know.'

Silence fell between them like a held breath. Emma looked away, heat suffusing her body, sticking her hair to the back of her neck, constricting her throat. She heard Leo shift his position.

'No, Emma.' His voice was pulled taut. 'There will be no more women. I am married to you now. I have made my vows, and I will respect them. Always.'

'You say that now, but—'

'No buts.' Cupping her jaw with one warm, strong hand, he lifted her chin until she had no choice but to fall into the drugging intimacy of his gaze. 'I will be totally faithful, in the same way as I expect you to be to me.'

Emma blinked hard. The idea of her ever being unfaithful to Leo was so ludicrous it was almost funny. She knew in her heart that she would never want another man. No one could ever match up to Leo. He would be her one and only lover. She could already picture herself, old and alone, Miss-Havishamlike, pining for the man she could never have. Maybe minus the wedding dress...

And yet Leo's declaration, the sheer intensity of his grey stare, did not match her bleak, chaste vision. It was controlled and commanding, as always, but provocative too, searching for some sort of confirmation.

'Well, of course,' she mumbled beneath her breath. 'That goes without saying.'

'Then we have a starting point to work from.' Like a switch flicked, Leo's mood changed to one of quiet intent. With his head on one side, he raised his hand, his thumb and forefinger tracing along her jawline with a caress so soft it was almost not there. But Emma's eyelids still flickered with the unwanted tremor, her skin blazing in the wake of his touch. 'It is incumbent on us both to try and make this commitment to one another work.'

'As long as it's all on your terms?' Emma dug around for the last of her defiance, which was being seriously undermined by a dangerous heat that was creeping over her every nerve.

The effect this man had on her was astonishing.

'Terms to be arranged.' The words were businesslike but his swift, assessing gaze anything but. 'Now...' All brisk authority again, he dropped his hand, shoving it into the pocket of his trousers to retrieve the car key. 'Are you going to accompany me back to the car, or am I going to have to carry you kicking and screaming?'

Emma screwed up her eyes, refusing to let that image permeate her brain.

She felt Leo slip his arm around her shoulder, taking advantage of her confusion, shepherding her forward. And as she found herself obediently sliding into the seat beside him, studiously avoiding his imperious profile as he started the car, she wondered for the umpteenth time how on earth she had ended up in this crazy situation. And, more importantly, how was she going to find the fight to survive living alongside this man?

Leo took the scan photograph out of his pocket and laid it flat on his desk. Only now he was alone in his office could he trust himself to look at it properly. Being in that claustrophobic consulting room had him shut down. The shock of seeing the beating heart of his baby punching emotion right through him. Hard and deep. Raw. Stealing his breath in a way he had never experienced before.

Something about the look of expectation on Emma's face had been the final straw, pushing him over the edge. His only option had been to get out, take some time to process what was happening. Deal with it.

Now he studied the row of images in meticulous detail, his finger tracing the baby's skull, its profile, the tiny jut of its nose. His son or daughter. He felt the muscles in his gut knot in response.

Once upon a time, having a child *had* been part of his life plan. Back when he'd assumed he would be the next Conte di Ravenino, when he had agreed to marry Cordelia Moretti, he had seen producing an heir as part of the job, a duty he would have performed with due diligence, like any other task necessary for the good of his family.

Fool that he was, even after the title had been so cruelly snatched away from him, a misguided sense of honour had seen him prepared to go ahead with their marriage. Leonardo Ravenino was a man of his word after all. He didn't let people down.

What an idiot!

He still squirmed with horror at the look on Cordelia's face when he had gone to see her with his noble reassurance. Surprise, panic even, quickly masked by a cool detachment. That wouldn't be necessary, she had briskly informed him. Different plans had been made. After a respectful period of separation she would, in fact, be marrying his brother Taddeo, the true Conte di Ravenino. *Had no one told him?*

No, no one had. Because he hadn't mattered any more.

Betrayed by his mother, let down by his fiancée, Leo had resolved there and then never to trust a woman again. Cordelia may have hurt his pride more than his heart, but he refused to ever be manipulated by the fairer sex again. From now on he would remain firmly single. No more engagements. No emotional ties or complications. And definitely no children. He had been adamant about that.

Now look at him. Once again, the course of his life had been changed by a woman. But this time the consequences were far more serious than hurt pride. More serious even than losing the principality. This was momentous.

Leo tore his eyes away from the images of his child, roughly raking a hand through his hair. His mind went back to Emma's furious outburst in the street earlier, tensing his muscles. The first time he had seen her temper, felt the flash of its fire. It had had a strange effect on him. Irritation, yes, but a sort of triumph, like her display of emotion had unlocked something between them, banishing his brooding mood. And arousal too—though that was never far from the surface with this woman.

But he would not allow Emma to think that having public tantrums meant getting her way. Or private ones, for that matter. He'd seen too many of them these past few years—accusations hurled at him from spurned lovers, women with quivering lips and flashing talons declaring what a bastard he was. Maybe they were right. Technically, they definitely were.

Emma's no-holds-barred article had certainly painted an ugly picture of him. Describing him like some modern-day Casanova, a philandering, heart-breaking womaniser, she hadn't held back with colourful adjectives, all delivered in that sanctimonious way that suggested she herself would never be taken in by such a man. That she was far too clever for that. Except of course she wasn't. Emma may have chosen to leave out the night they had spent together, but that didn't mean it hadn't happened. She couldn't erase the twist of their limbs, the collision of heated skin, the sweet deep shudders that had racked her body, culminating in the screaming of his name. No matter how much she wanted to. And she certainly couldn't erase the baby growing in her womb.

Then there were the toxic references to his background, her veiled suppositions about the Principality of Ravenino. That he had been stripped of his title because of some sort of infidelity, betrayed his fiancée, embarrassed his father, deemed unfit to rule because of his debauched behaviour. She had got it all wrong, of course, but that was no consolation.

He had had no choice but to pick up the phone and demand that Emma Quinn be fired from her position at the *Paladin* with immediate effect. He had been perfectly within his rights. Had he chosen to he could have brought the whole damned newspaper to its knees. But the dark truth was it was Emma alone he had wanted to punish. For holding a mirror up to his hedonistic lifestyle, reflecting an image he didn't want to see.

But even more so for having the audacity to poke about in his past, for trying to uncover what he'd been so determined to leave behind. Just the thought of her picking over the bones of his life felt like the worst sort of betrayal. Gleefully piecing together all the snippets of information she could find, the more heartbreaking, the more tragic the better, so she could cobble together that nasty piece of salacious trash.

At the time fury had overridden any other

emotion. But time had turned that fury into a small, hard ball. It still sat within him, but no longer carried the same weight. Events had overtaken them. Other emotions had crept in. And one of them was guilt. For the way he had treated Emma that fateful night, and the way he was treating her now. An unwelcome visitor, it took Leo by surprise every time it sank its claws into him. And he didn't like it. Not one bit. It made him feel weak. Exposed. It meant he had to redouble his efforts to hold her at bay.

Which was why he had had to shut her down earlier, silence her chatter. His new wife had to learn that the more something mattered, the less he was going to talk about it. Circumstances had brought them together, but that did not give her the right to get inside his head. He would provide every possible comfort for Emma and the baby. Complete security. And complete faithfulness. But that was it.

Leo sat back in his chair, swinging it to one side, staring unseeing at the sprawling city of Milan far below. Everything had happened so fast he had never even considered the moral implications of his marriage. But he'd meant what he'd said. He would be totally faithful. Judging by the crazy way his body reacted to her, Emma was more than enough to fulfil his needs. When the time came, he would make damned sure he fulfilled hers. It would be his pleasure. Literally.

Physically he didn't doubt they could make this work. But emotionally Emma had to realise what she was working with. A man who didn't do feelings and who certainly didn't do love. She only needed to go back to her own article to find the truth. Leo Ravenino was a man with a heart of stone.

And the sooner she realised that the better.

CHAPTER NINE

IT WAS LATE by the time Leo arrived back at the villa. Work, when he had finally been able to put his mind to it, had provided temporary relief from the roar in his head.

There was no sign of Emma when he walked into the salon. Neither was she in the library or out on the terrace. A creeping sense of unease flooded over him as he paced from one empty room to the next. Where the hell was she?

Impatient feet took him in search of Maria, who informed him she had seen the *signora* less than an hour ago when she had returned her supper tray to the kitchen. Apparently, she had told the cook she was going to take a walk around the grounds before dark.

Leo slowly let the air out of his lungs. He needed to calm down, stop overreacting. Stop letting his wife's slender hands from metaphorically grabbing him round the neck.

He found her down by the lake, sitting on a bench that was catching the last amber rays of sunshine. Speaking into her phone, she hadn't heard Leo approaching and he paused, listening. It seemed to be an intense conversation, judging by the way Emma was twisting her legs around each other, her head bowed so that her hair fell forward, obscuring her face.

'Well, it's not as if you would have come to the wedding.'

Leo edged closer.

'But that's just it, I didn't want to be talked out of it. Leo and I both agreed we wanted to marry before the baby was born.'

She twisted a strand of hair tightly around her finger.

'I know that, Mum. I know there are alternatives. I've lived with the alternatives all my life. But I needed to do what was right for me. And for the baby.'

The catch in her voice carried on the air, stiffening Leo's spine.

'I'm not asking you to understand. I'm just telling you because I thought you'd want to know.'

Leo had heard enough. Throwing back his shoulders, he stepped out of the shadows.

Emma jumped, the phone almost falling

from her hand. Glaring at Leo, she ended the call with a rushed goodbye.

'Has no one ever told you it's rude to listen in to other people's conversations?' She pushed back her shoulders.

Leo ignored her comment, sitting down beside her, making her edge further away.

'Your mother, I take it?'

'Yes.' Emma looked down at her fingernails.

'Passing on her congratulations, no doubt.' Sarcasm masked the vitriol he felt for that woman. Emma's account of the way she had treated her still burned a hole inside him.

'Not exactly. She doesn't believe in marriage. Especially to capitalist billionaires.'

Leo made a dismissive noise in his throat. He didn't give a damn what this hateful woman thought of him and his way of life, but the fact that she couldn't support her daughter really got under his skin.

There was a beat of silence.

'Why do you do it?' Leo turned to look at his wife. Wearing a bright yellow cotton dress, she made him think of sunshine. But her mood was grey.

'Do what?'

'Why do you let your mother get to you like this?'

'I don't know what you mean.'

'Yes, you do, Emma, you know exactly what I mean.'

Emma shrugged. 'Because she's my mother, I guess.'

'And that's enough, is it? That gives her the right to treat you like dirt for the rest of her life and for you to accept it?'

'No, of course not.' Flustered, Emma looked down at her lap. 'And I never said she treated me like dirt.'

She hadn't had to, it was obvious. Leo glowered into the fading light, his gaze travelling across the lake, at the golden rays rippling across the water, the darting shapes of the low swooping swifts.

'Well, I'm just saying it might be nice if your mother started to show you some respect. That's all.'

Emma's startled look twisted something inside him. Was it really such a shock that he was sticking up for her? It occurred to him that maybe she had never had anyone on her side. That she was still fighting her own battles now. And he had done nothing to help with that.

They hadn't exactly parted on good terms earlier in the day. The journey back to Villa Magenta had been conducted largely in silence, Emma staring resolutely ahead, her profile, when Leo had sneaked the occasional glance, very still, framed by the curtain of brown hair. Dropping her at the steps to the villa, he hadn't even gone in with her, turning the car and heading straight back to his office in the city. His parting words that he would see her later had been ignored in her hurry to get out of the car. His actions had seemed reasonable at the time. Now they felt harsh. Petulant even.

'And if she can't do that, you need to cut her out of your life.' He drove home his point with ruthless conviction.

But Emma's gaze had sharpened. 'Like you have with your family?'

Well, that would teach him. By trying to help, by starting to *care*, he had fallen straight into her trap. Suddenly his wife was no longer a wronged daughter but a prying journalist again.

'Still looking for a scoop, Emma?' his voice growled.

'No.' She shook her head. 'I'm not asking as a journalist. I no longer have that job, if you recall. I am asking as your wife. The mother of your child.'

'Yes, I do recall.' Bitterness tore at his voice. 'I recall the pack of lies you wrote

about me, about my reasons for leaving Ravenino.'

'Then why don't you tell me the true story?'
Her voice was soft but determined, designed
to throw a cloak over his anger. But it didn't
work. Especially when it was followed up by
her next question. 'Why did you never inherit
the title of Conte di Ravenino?'

Just hearing Emma use that title, *a title
that should have been his*, felt like sandpa-
per scraping across his skin. His reaction
was irrational, he knew that, but Ravenino
had long since stolen the rational part of his
brain. No matter how hard he had tried to ignore the place, to bury his resentment beneath
the distractions of work, women, more work,
more women, it still pulsed inside him like
an angry beast, red and raw and very much
alive. It occurred to Leo that Emma too was
capable of robbing him of rationality. This
was a bad combination. He needed to shut
her down. Right away.

'My family is dead to me.' He turned his
profile on her. 'That's all you need to know.'

'But why?' Still she pushed. Against the
wall built of years of resentment.

A bruised silence fell between them, the
sky darkening along with the mood.

'Because some things are best left to rot in

the dark.' The effort to remain rational was costing him dear. Even then he had said more than he'd meant to.

'And some are better brought out to the light.'

'What's this, Emma?' His dismissive snarl was intended to wound. 'Some homespun pearls of wisdom from the little book of love and peace? Careful, your hippie roots are starting to show.'

'So what if they are?' Far from leaving her cowed, it seemed the more he turned against her, the stronger she came back at him. 'At least I had the courage to share my background with you. At least I didn't pretend it didn't exist.'

'Che diavolo.' Leo's curse split the air. Pitching away from her, he dragged a hand across the back of his neck. 'Very well. You win.' He aggressively pushed back his shoulders. 'My mother was a manipulative, adulterous liar. There, is that good enough for you? Does that satisfy your thirst for scandal?'

'I'm not looking for scandal. Just the truth.'

'I think you will find they are one and the same.' Slowly he turned back to face her. 'I spent the first twenty-eight years of my life assuming I would inherit the title of Conte di

Ravenino, only to discover just before my father died that I had no entitlement to it at all. Because I am not a true Ravenino.'

Emma blinked against the force of his words. 'But why? I don't understand.'

'*Certo*, that's the name on my birth certificate, the only name I've got, but Alberto Ravenino was not my real father.'

'You are the result of a love affair that your mother had with someone else?' He could see her trying to put the pieces together.

Leo gave a dismissive laugh. 'What a romantic you are, Emma. I appreciate your attempt to make my conception sound like the result of a romantic tryst, but in all probability, it was just as likely to have been a sordid fumble in a back alley somewhere. And no doubt a great inconvenience to all concerned. My mother duped Alberto into thinking he was my father. Lied to him all their married life. Only on his deathbed did he face up to his suspicions. The idea of meeting his maker while carrying the burden of doubt must have focussed his mind.'

So she had got it all wrong. Emma twisted her hands in her lap as silence settled between them, muffling the night. All those awful things she had written about him, that he had lost his birthright because of his own immoral behaviour were completely untrue. He had been wronged. By his family and then by her. Heat flushed her cheeks as she turned to him.

'I'm so sorry, Leo.'

Immediately Leo stiffened. 'I don't want your sympathy.'

No, of course he didn't. Leo Ravenino was all about strength, power, self-control. Sympathy was for the weak. For lesser beings than himself.

'I'm not offering sympathy.' She edged closer nervously. 'I want to apologise for those things I wrote about you. I'm very sorry.'

Leo's shrug did nothing to assuage her guilt.

'If I had known the truth, I would never have—'

'Spare me the excuses. I'm not interested.'

'But I want you to understand.' Shame lanced through her, choking her throat. 'I didn't know you then!'

'You still don't know me, Emma.' His cold, clinical voice was designed to flatten all emotion. 'I doubt you ever will.'

Emma bit down on her lip, determined to halt its tremor. He was right, they didn't know one another. Despite the intimacy they had shared, the consequences and the actions they'd had to take because of those consequences, they were little more than strangers. Emma had hoped, assumed even, that gradually they would learn about each other, learn to trust. *Maybe even to love.* But Leo had no such goal. Instead he was using the wall of his past like a barrier to keep her out.

Taking a breath, she turned away to look at the view, Leo's proud, resolute profile making it clear there was no point in prolonging her apology or offering anything else to try and make amends.

She forced her hands to unclasp, and instinctively they spread over her stomach, cradling the invisible baby. Their baby. Despite Leo's harsh manner, his hurtful refusal to let her into his life, she couldn't help but feel for him. For what he had suffered. Speaking with such bitter passion about his mother and the man he had thought to be his father, he had exposed just how hurt he had been. How wounded he still was. His contempt for the man who had fathered him, who hadn't been honourable enough to face up to his responsibilities, still pulsed like a living beast.

Emma was learning that Leo was all about honour. If you cut him open it would be written through him like a stick of rock. He may

have broken many a woman's heart, but he
didn't cheat. He was a hugely successful businessman, but he'd made his billions fairly,
through hard work and intuition. And if you
were foolish enough to get someone pregnant…you did the decent thing. Straight away.
No questions asked. No matter how much
your life might be inconvenienced by it.

Unlike her own father, he would never
abandon their child.

His strong moral values should have been
a comfort to Emma—they *were* a comfort.
She knew that in practical terms Leo would
be there for them for ever, come what may.
She knew that they would want for nothing.
But she also knew that she was walking on
increasingly dangerous ground. Because the
further she tunnelled inside Leo's head, the
more she managed to discover about him, the
more vulnerable it made her. Inch by inch,
Leo Ravenino was winding his way around
her heart.

She shifted in her seat, sitting on her hands
to keep them still. Beside her Leo had gone
quiet, staring sullenly into the night. But beneath the dark glower, the simmering hostility, some basic instinct made her want to try
and ease his burden.

'So you don't know who your real father is?' She spoke cautiously into the dark.

'No. Neither do I care.' Leo's jaw clenched. 'Any man who turns his back on his unborn child, lets him be raised by another man, doesn't deserve to be called a father.'

'You don't know what the circumstances were at the time. Your father may not even have known of your existence. Maybe your mother had her reasons for not telling him.'

'There are no excuses. What my mother did was beneath contempt and the man I thought to be my father was too weak to do anything about it.'

'Yes, but—'

'No buts.' Leo's dark silhouette stiffened, his voiced laced with irritation. 'Why do you persist in trying to see the good in people when clearly there isn't any? My mother, your mother. By trying to justify their behaviour you are merely demeaning yourself.'

His words were designed to hurt but Emma refused to feel them.

'And if I look for the good in you?'

'Then you are a fool.' The reply whistled back, as cold as a bullet.

Leo turned away, but not before Emma had caught the flash of something raw before the night shadows took hold, sculpting his face like stone. And despite his rebuttal, she found herself reaching for him again.

'I'm just saying we all make mistakes.' Her hand found his arm, which was tightly folded across his chest. She felt his muscles flex beneath her touch, but he didn't pull away. 'It's easy to make bad decisions that we later regret.'

'Yeah, well, in my case this particular *mistake* meant that I lost everything.'

'Not everything, surely?' She could feel his skin beneath his shirtsleeve, warm, hostile.

'The Principality of Ravenino, the title of Conte, my home, my job—the role I had been groomed for all my life. Is that enough for you? Oh, and my fiancée. We mustn't forget her.'

Emma stilled. 'Cordelia?'

'Yes, Cordelia. Full marks, Emma, for remembering her name.' A long-held bitterness scoured his voice. 'But just to put the record straight, the engagement was not broken off because of my infidelity. It ended on the result of a single DNA test, along with the rest of my future as I knew it.'

Emma swallowed hard. *Cordelia Moretti.* She thought back to the images she had come across when doing her research on Leo. The wedding photos of Cordelia's marriage to

Taddeo, Leo's younger brother, now the Conte di Ravenino. A fine, sophisticated woman with an aquiline nose, her dark hair swept back into a sleek chignon, diamond earrings dangling against the long sweep of her neck. She was everything that Emma wasn't.

At the time Emma had assumed Cordelia had been wronged by Leo, that he had treated her badly. Broken up with her. Broken her heart for all she knew. Now she saw how she had got everything the wrong way round. It was Leo who had been the victim. Had he also been the one with the broken heart? Was that why he still hurt so badly?

She let go of Leo's arm, feeling something coming apart inside her, something she couldn't control. No wonder he had never shown any feelings for her. It all made sense now. She could never compete with a woman like Cordelia. Fevered thoughts piled one on top of the other, each more torturous than the last.

Oh, God, why did this have to be so hard?

'Nothing to say, Emma? No more questions you want answered? More details of my tragic past you would like to pick over?'

'No.' She fought against the swell of emotion pressing down on her chest. She fought with everything she'd got. She fought so hard it hurt.

Because she couldn't carry on like this, being slowly torn apart by Leo. She could never be Cordelia. She could never make Leo love her. But she was his wife. She was carrying his child. They were tied together for ever. So she had two choices. Either let herself be crushed with misery or stand up and fight.

She pulled back a little but refused to spare herself the weight of his gaze. She could do this, she told herself sternly. She was stronger than she thought. From the age of sixteen she had been on her own, working so hard to keep a roof over her head, food on the table, studying like crazy to get some qualifications, fighting for a career. She had moved countries to marry a man who was almost a stranger, come to terms with her shock pregnancy.

She had done all this without collapsing in a heap or running screaming for the hills. She wasn't going to start now. Fate had played some strange tricks on her, but fate didn't hold all the cards. She did have agency. She just had to use it.

'Actually, yes.' She changed her mind. 'I do have another question. What do you want from our relationship, Leo?' She addressed him boldly, her eyes never leaving his face. The question took on a force of its own, spilling out in the silence that followed.

She saw the column of Leo's throat move on a swallow, his lips firm, then soften, before he finally spoke. 'I thought we had already established this.'

'No, we haven't. At least not to my satisfaction.' Emma held her nerve. Even if it felt like jumping on board a runaway train. 'What do you want from me? What is my role to be?'

'My wife. The mother of my child.' His eyes narrowed to dangerous slits of steel. 'Surely these are not difficult concepts to grasp.'

'Your lover?' Emma spoke the words like a dare, quickly, before her nerve failed her. 'Am I to share your bed?'

'Do you want to share my bed, Emma?' He turned the question around so fast she had no time to prepare for it. Like a mirror swung round to face her, she saw her own startled expression.

'I... I would like some clarity...going forward...'

'Clarity?' He reached out, his finger gently tracing a line along her lips, as if reading her question like Braille. 'Is that what you want?' With his head on one side he silently regarded her, like an interesting specimen. 'Or do you want sex, Emma? Hot. Wild. Passionate sex?'

Emma gave a sharp gasp.

'Because I can do that…' He whispered the words slowly, his thumb moving to stroke her cheek, his head lowering almost imperceptibly until his lips hovered just above hers. 'If that's what you want.'

Like a curse cast over her, or a drug she was addicted to, she didn't just want it—she yearned for it, ached for it. She wanted Leo so badly at this moment she would have traded her soul. Her next breath.

'Say you want it, Emma.'

'I… I want it.'

His lips finally came down on hers, hot and firm. A commanding kiss that drove through Emma, turning everything soft and sweet. Calling to the growing ache in her core. Carrying away her fears and doubts, pushing them blissfully out of reach. At least for now. Because nothing felt more right than this.

The kiss ended and their arms loosened but still neither of them moved. Struggling to find a breath, to steady the thud of her heart, Emma looked into Leo's eyes, his wild stare pulling everything tight inside her. She took another gasp of air, air that was full of the scent of him, heady and potent. Her aching need for him screamed from every nerve, drowning the small voice that tried to tell her she needed to be very careful. Because being in Leo's arms felt like coming home. Like only he could make her happiness complete. And that was a very dangerous path to walk.

'I cannot be the man you want me to be, Emma.' Almost as if he could read her mind, Leo's voice was low. 'You need to know that.'

With a surge of boldness Emma rose to her feet, standing on tiptoe, her hand shaking as she slid it over the hard, flexing muscles of his chest, past the buckle of his belt, until it found the swell of his erection. She did have agency. She did have power. She refused to be the victim.

'Then I will take the man you are.'

Leo stared into her beautiful face, at the determined line of her mouth, her eyes dark with desire. Reckless hunger pounded through him hot and hard. Like a dam about to burst he couldn't hold it back any longer. He had tried to do right by her, tried to make her see that man he was. But she had turned his warning into a promise. The words, falling softly from her lips, the most erotic thing he had ever heard. *I will take the man you are*.

So be it. He would give her that man.

Taking hold of her arms, he linked them

behind his neck, tugging her towards him, her hair falling over her shoulders as she tipped her head back. His lips found hers again, the wet heat of her mouth slamming hot, hard arousal to every part of his body. Running his hands over her shoulder blades to the small of her back, he let out a guttural moan as his pounding erection met her soft curves. And when Emma returned the sound, writhing against him, Leo deepened the kiss, shifting his position so that his thigh was nudging between her legs. The dam had burst now. There was no going back. He had been waiting for this moment for too long. Far too long.

They fell apart with a shared gasp of breath. Unable to wait another minute, another second, Leo reached for her hand, hurrying them back through the gardens, tall black shadows marking their way before the villa loomed into view, brightly lit windows glowing against the dark. He opened the back door, pausing only for a second to glance at his wife, her tousled hair, her shining eyes. So beautiful. Tightening his grip on her hand, he silently led her along the long corridor that led to the vast kitchen, flicking the overhead spotlights on then off again, the brightness too much after the darkness outside.

He turned to kiss her again, relishing the

bite of pain as Emma threaded her fingers into his hair, digging her nails into his scalp. With his hands cradling her head, the softness of her hair spread over his fingers, flowing over his wrists, like a river of silk.

Setting his hips in a rhythmic sway, he pulled her tightly against him, her eager response, the way she arched into his body driving him on. Driving him crazy. His hands slid over her bottom, bunching up the floaty fabric of her short summer dress until he was underneath, slipping his fingers under the skimpy panties, seeking her slick, wet core.

Emma gave a twitch of pleasure at his first light touch, which soon turned to a guttural moan as his fingers worked faster, more deliberately, his own need a bright light behind his eyes as he felt the thrill of her coming closer and closer to orgasm. With one arm locked around her waist, he backed her against the wall, his focus entirely on giving her the maximum pleasure, instinctively knowing what she liked.

And when her sharp gasp told him she was there, he covered her mouth with his own, his breath hot and fierce as he absorbed the shudder of her release, felt it ripple through his body, almost as if it was his own.

Which was not going to be far behind.

For a moment they stood there, their breathing ragged as they gazed into one another's eyes. Never had Leo seen a more beautiful sight. All soft curves and warm skin, her eyes bright, her cheeks flushed, Emma called to him on some deeper level. Somewhere he had never been before.

But if he didn't get a grip, they weren't going to make it to a bedroom. Not that he minded. Such was his frenzy, his aching need to make love to Emma, he would have happily performed there and then, on top of the granite worktops or up against the vast shiny fridge he wasn't sure he had ever opened. But Emma deserved better.

Taking hold of her hand, he laced his fingers tightly through hers. He was going to get them upstairs, into his bedroom and into his bed if it was the last thing he did. He was going to make love to her, passionately, crazily, with everything he had. Until the ache in his soul was satisfied. Until he had made her his once and for all. Until he had finally found peace.

CHAPTER TEN

'*BENE…BENE.*' BEATRICE lifted up the pasta, inspecting it closely as Emma rolled it through the machine for the umpteenth time. 'You are definitely getting the 'ang of this.'

Emma smiled. Queen of the kitchen, Beatrice had taken some persuading to let her anywhere near her pasta machine, so the pressure had been on from the start. Making the dough had been stressful enough, Beatrice barking instructions in rapid Italian or broken English, both equally unintelligible, elbowing Emma out of the way when she did something particularly terrible, as if the sky might come crashing down because of it.

Nevertheless, Emma was enjoying herself. And she adored Beatrice. Small and plump, her smooth cheeks often dusted with flour, they reminded Emma of the soft balls of dough she so lovingly created. The mother of six grown-up children, Beatrice had been widowed ten years ago, forced to go back to work when her useless, incompetent husband had died leaving her penniless. You would never get her to admit it, but she loved her job at Villa Magenta. She even loved all the high-tech equipment, boasting about it to her friends. 'I say to Agnesia, *You no have the steam oven? You livin' in the Dark Ages.*'

'You think it is ready for the filling?' Emma stopped turning the handle of the machine.

'*Sì...sì...*'

They were making prosciutto and ricotta ravioli, Leo's favourite according to Beatrice, who seemed to know the food preferences of anyone who had ever crossed her path.

Emma had been living at the villa for two months now, two months that had stirred up such a complicated mix of emotions she didn't know how to begin to untangle them. What's more, she didn't even want to. Because to examine their relationship, to try and understand the sexual relationship they had embarked on, in all its intense, vivid glory, meant examining herself. Something Emma was studiously avoiding doing.

Starting that evening down by the lake, when they had finally fallen upon each other like starving beasts, tumbling into bed and making love with wild and deeply sensual craving, there had been no going back. Like some sort of crazy addiction, a mad, hedonistic ride of pleasure, it was hot and wild and raw. And totally uncontrollable.

It could happen anywhere, at any time, but mostly Leo would come to her bed late at night, running his fingers down her spine or moving her hair aside to kiss the nape of her neck. And Emma would find her body instantly on fire, her hands reaching for him, urgent, desperate, to take her to that place only he could take her, make her feel something only he could.

She had quickly learned how to give pleasure as well as receive. An innocent virgin no more, she had done things that made her blush in the cold light of day, made her shiver with excitement at the thought of repeating them. Like taking Leo in her mouth, closing her lips around the silky hot girth of him, revelling in the way she could make him feel. She loved turning him on like that. It was empowering, life enhancing.

But sexual intimacy was as far as it went. In all other ways their relationship was as sterile as it had ever been. Worse if anything. The wall that Leo seemed so determined to surround himself with grew taller and more impregnable with every week that passed. Like he was building it up, brick by brick.

On the surface he was polite, enquiring after her health, how her day had gone. But it was a distracted courtesy, like he was keeping her at arm's length, his mind already moving onto something else, something more worthy of his valuable time. There was a distinct lack of familiarity between them, any closeness solely restricted to sex. No cosying up on the sofa, chilling out together, enjoying each other's company, the way normal couples did. They had never even spent the entire night together.

Waiting until after she had fallen asleep, or using the excuse of work, always more work, Leo would extricate himself from her arms and disappear into the night. The bed beside her empty in the morning, the crumpled sheets, the scent of his body all that was left of the intimacy they had shared. A damning indictment of what could never be.

But it wasn't like he hadn't tried to warn her. *I cannot be the man you want me to be.*

Alone again, his words would come back to haunt Emma. But she only had herself to blame. She was the one who had initiated this shift in their relationship. She was a hopeless case, she knew that. Like a dog chasing her own tail, going round and round and getting nowhere. Ordering herself not to get emotionally involved but constantly obsessing over him. Determined to mirror his cool demeanour but thinking about Leo all the time. Dreaming of him. Falling in love with him…

No matter how hard Emma tried to ignore that traitorous word, it kept coming back to haunt her, niggling away at the back of her head, threatening to fall unbidden from her lips if she wasn't careful. So she made sure she was on her guard at all times. She would rather saw off her own legs than let Leo see as much as a chink of how she felt about him. He had made his feeling towards her quite clear—at least his lack of them. It was up to her to deal with the situation as it was. No matter how much it hurt.

'*Buonasera.*' Standing in the kitchen doorway, the room was suddenly full of Leo's presence, the air thick with the pull of him. Wearing a dark suit, the jacket slung over his shoulder and held by one crooked finger, his grey eyes flicked between Beatrice and Emma. 'What is going on here?'

'Beatrice is teaching me how to make pasta.' Emma gestured to the perfectly shaped squares of deliciousness, steadfastly ignoring the thumping of her heart. 'Prosciutto and ricotta ravioli.'

'My favourite.' Leo raised a dark brow a fraction and Beatrice gave Emma a complacent smile. 'I'll just take a quick shower and then we can eat.'

Supper was taken out on the terrace as usual. Even though summer had turned to autumn, the evenings were still gloriously warm and Emma for one was relieved the searing temperatures had dropped.

'Delizioso,' Leo declared, touching a napkin to his lips before scrunching it up and laying it on the table. 'Beatrice has taught you well. We will make an Italian mama out of you yet.'

Emma smiled. 'I don't know about that, but I love spending time with her. She's a fantastic cook. Where did you find her?'

'A restaurant I used to frequent in Milan. The food was great, so I went into the kitchen and told her to come and work for me.'

'Just like that?'

'Sì. I always find a direct approach works best.'

That was *so* Leo. You saw what you wanted, then you made it happen. Except, of course, when the circumstances were completely out of your control. Like finding out you are not the legitimate heir of the principality you had been raised to rule. Emma could see how hard that must have been for a proud man like him to accept. It was still there, held inside him, like a poisonous canker. But any attempts to broach the subject again, maybe try and talk it through with him, had been firmly shut down.

'Did you know that one of her sons, Giuseppe, has got a new job working for a big pharmaceutical company?' Emma speared a piece of ravioli. 'Beatrice is thrilled because their youngest child has some health problems that have been putting a terrible strain on the family's finances.'

'Yes, I heard.'

Something about Leo's guarded response made Emma suspicious and she looked up. 'You wouldn't have had anything to do with that, would you?'

'Put it this way…' Leo raised his wine glass to his lips, hooded eyes regarding Emma over the rim '… I like to reward my loyal staff if I can.'

'And their families.'

'And their families,' Leo repeated, setting down his glass. 'We Italians are all about

families, you should know that.' The grey
eyes glittered.

Yes, Emma did know that. It was the reason she was here, after all. *The sole reason.*
And that thought stuck like a barb in her skin.
No matter how much she tried to justify the
bizarre terms of their relationship, tell herself
that this was the way it was, the way it would
always be, it was still so hard to accept.

She took a sip of water, carefully replacing
her glass. She could sense that Leo was already itching to go. Manners prevented him
from leaving the table until Emma had finished, but that didn't stop his foot from jig-
gling under the table, his fingers drumming
very lightly on the top. Well, tonight he would
have to wait.

'We have had a lot more applications from
journalists on the website today.' She searched
for his attention. 'The standard is very high.'

'Bene.' Leo surreptitiously looked at his
watch.

'I'm confident we are going to get some
really good people on board.'

'I'm sure you will.'

Emma sighed. Bored with sitting around
with nothing to do, she had asked Leo if she
could get involved with some of the many
charities that Raven Enterprises supported.

But in typical Leo fashion he had escalated her request, suggesting they started a foundation in her name.

It was an exciting idea, if a bit daunting. Deciding she would like to use her experience in journalism somehow, and maybe focus on youth unemployment and homelessness—if nothing else, living at Villa Magenta had made her aware of just what a privileged life she was leading—she had taken these ideas to Leo and he had made them happen. Constructive journalism was key, he told her, taking a solution-focussed approach.

And so the foundation Read All About It had been born. Financial support for young journalists to work with charities and highlight the issues they faced. The idea was simple but brilliant.

Heading up a small team of people, Emma was really enjoying the challenge, the feeling she was making a difference. But there was disappointment too, because Leo had dissociated himself from the project as soon as it had been launched.

'Would you like to look over some of the figures?' She already knew the answer, but she couldn't help herself.

'No need. The foundation is in your name, you have complete control.'

'But it's your money.' She persisted. 'Don't you want to make sure it is being spent wisely?'

'The lawyers will do that. That's their job.'

Emma sighed. It was great that he trusted her to just get on with it, but the way he was distancing himself from any involvement felt like he was distancing her. Still further.

'Okay, if you're sure.' She put down her fork. 'Have you finished?'

'Sì, grazie.'

'Then I will get the dessert.' With a determined air, Emma rose, collecting up the bowls.

'Dessert?' The surprise in his voice was not exactly encouraging. To be fair, she had never seen him eat anything sweet.

'Yes. Beatrice asked me to show her how to make a traditional English pudding. I didn't have exactly the right ingredients, so I had to make do.'

'Well, I look forward to seeing the result.' *No, he didn't.*

'Wait there.' Emma stretched out an arm, as if to physically prevent him from escaping. She was determined not to let him cut and run. 'I won't be a moment.'

The pudding, as Emma removed it from the oven, was not all she had hoped it might be. Rather more solid than she'd intended, it was distinctly burnt on the top. And there was no sign of Beatrice to save it. Presumably she had abandoned it and Emma to their fate. Still, ever the optimist, Emma decided she could blag it. It wasn't as if Leo knew how it was supposed to look.

'Ta-da!' She placed it on the table before him.

'Is this a family recipe?' Leo regarded it with suspicion.

Emma didn't have any family recipes. She hadn't had that sort of family.

'No, it's more like an old-fashioned English dish. But these retro puddings are all the rage now.' She tried to dig the spoon in to serve Leo a portion, but it was surprisingly difficult.

'Need any help?'

'No, no.' Emma ignored the smile in his voice, leaning forward to get some more leverage. 'There you are.' She placed the bowl in front of him.

'Interesting.' Leo turned a burnt corner over to peer underneath. 'What is this delicacy called?'

'Bread and butter pudding.' Emma popped a bit in her mouth. It tasted as bad as it looked.

'It was meant to be made with slices of white bread, but I had to use ciabatta.'

'Very ingenious.' His jaw worked with exaggerated force.

'But I'm not sure it's quite the same.'

'Possibly not.' Leo raised laughing eyes to meet hers, a curve shaping the firm lines of his mouth.

Emma looked down before her face betrayed her. Leo smiled so little that when he did it was like a full-on assault to the heart.

'It's disgusting, isn't it?' She risked looking up at him again.

'Assolutamente disgustoso.' He stuck in his fork which remained standing defiantly upright. 'Though all is not lost. I dare say it could be used to fill some gaps in the walls.'

'Oi!' With a laugh Emma balled up her napkin and threw it at him but it missed, knocking over his wine glass, sending red wine spraying over Leo's shirt. 'Oh, God, I'm sorry.' She rushed round to pat at his shirt but immediately he was on his feet, trapping her in his arms. 'You need to take that off right away. It will stain.'

'Or you could do it for me, *cara*?' He placed her hands on his chest, where his heart thudded beneath the damp fabric. Immediately Emma felt the familiar coil of desire, the pulsing clench of her core.

Her fingers started to work at the buttons, driven on by slumbering eyes darkening with desire. But their progress was halted by the persistent buzz of Leo's phone in his trouser pocket.

'*Aspetta*. Wait.' He slid his hand down between them. 'Let me turn this off.'

But that never happened. One glance at the screen and Emma saw his features pull tight, his whole body stiffen. '*Mi scusi*. I have to take this.'

It wasn't even a proper apology. More a distracted mutter that he didn't care if she heard or not. With his shoulders high he turned, his stride wide as he left the room with the phone clamped to his ear.

So that was it then. With a heavy sigh, Emma watched him go. Once again, she had been abandoned in favour of whatever deal he was doing, a business negotiation that was clearly far more important than she was. She glanced back across the table, at the offending pudding curling up before her eyes. Her gaze rose to the horizon, looking for inspiration, strength, a miracle—she didn't know which.

Rising to her feet, she went over to the sunbed further along the terrace, picking up the book she had left there earlier. Stretching out on the padded cushions, she found her page. It looked as if this was the only company she would be having this evening.

'Emma?'

She must have closed her eyes for a minute because the book on her lap had fallen to the floor. She leaned to pick it up. 'Yes?'

'Something has come up.' Leo strode towards her, his silhouette dark, forbidding. 'I have to go away.'

'Oh, right.' Emma collected herself, smoothing down her hair, drawing up her knees. She could tell from the tone of his voice that this was no ordinary business trip.

'I will be gone for some time.'

'When you say some time…'

'I don't know exactly. As long as it takes.' Impatience simmered in his tone.

'And when will you be leaving on this trip of indeterminate length?' She hid her despondency behind a mask of sarcasm.

'Tonight. Straight away.'

'Tonight?!' Emma swung her legs over the edge of the sunbed. 'But it's my twenty-week scan tomorrow. Surely whatever it is can wait until after that?'

'No, Emma, this can't wait.' His jaw was set as firmly as his words.

'But—'

'It's not as if I need to be there, Emma. You are the one that is pregnant.'

His words were like a shot to the heart. Like he was tearing her apart, bit by bit. There was no arguing with his merciless logic, but that didn't make it hurt any less.

'Very well. I'll see you when I see you, I guess.' She opened her book again, making a great show of finding a page she wasn't going to be reading. Anything to try and hide the hurt clawing its way to her throat.

'I will ring you in due course when I have a clearer idea of the length of my stay.'

'Fine.' She bent back the spine of the paperback. 'Whatever.'

She heard him take a few steps away, then stop.

'Indulging in petulant behaviour is not going to help the situation, Emma.'

Very deliberately, Emma placed the book beside her and lifted her face to meet his.

'I didn't realise there was a "situation".' She fought back with everything she had. 'How could I when you haven't told me where you are going or the reason for your trip?'

'Ravenino.' He forced the word through clenched teeth. 'I have to return to Ravenino.'

Emma stared at him in astonishment. That was the last place she had expected him to say.

'It's my brother. He's had an accident.'

'Oh, I'm sorry, Leo!' Immediately on her feet, Emma rushed towards the solid wall of Leo's cool restraint, all petulance gone. 'Is it serious?'

'Head injuries. He fell off a horse. He's in an induced coma.' The unemotional information was delivered in bullet points.

'Oh, no! Of course you must go to him straight away.'

'I'm not going to sit by his bedside, Emma.' Irritation growled in his voice. 'They need me to take over the running of the principality. Cordelia is insistent that I'm the only person that can do it.'

Cordelia. Just her name on Leo's lips produced a sharp jab of jealousy.

'So that was Cordelia, was it?' Emma asked casually. 'On the phone?'

'*Sì.*' Distracted, Leo looked down at another message that had buzzed in. 'The jet has been put on standby. I need to leave for the airport.'

Emma swallowed down the horrible surge of jealousy. So Leo's assertion that he would never visit Ravenino again had been reversed by a single click of his ex-fiancée's elegant fingers. But this was an emergency, Emma reminded herself. Her own father had died in a riding accident, what if Leo's brother suffered the same fate? This was no time for petty jealousies. A sudden idea came to her.

'Why don't I come with you?'

Leo looked at her in surprise. 'To Ravenino?'

Yes, of course to Ravenino. Where else?

'Yes.' She kept up the bravado. 'I can postpone the scan for a week or so.'

'What would be the benefit in that?'

'Well, I would love to see where you come from and—'

'This is not a little holiday, Emma. I have a job to do. I don't need the encumbrance of a pregnant wife tagging along.'

Emma stilled, watching the wave of hurt coming towards her , crashing over her like a tsunami, dragging her under, drowning her breath.

She turned, her feet taking her back across the terrace, away from him. Tears choked her throat, but her eyes remained dry. She stared ahead, trying not to think, trying to hold the misery at bay. At least until he had gone.

Behind her Leo made a gruff sound in his throat. She heard him coming towards her and her shoulders stiffened, her whole body following suit, going rigid with tension. She couldn't do this. Not any more. Moving further away, she forced her vocal cords into action.

'Just go, Leo.' Her weary words floated into the night. 'Just go.'

CHAPTER ELEVEN

'THE QUARTERLY FINANCIAL budget projection needs to be finalised.' The secretary swiped at the tablet in his hand. 'The record of the legislative assembly agreed. And don't forget you have a meeting with the French ambassador on Tuesday.'

Leo nodded, dismissing his secretary, relieved the morning briefing was over.

He spanned a hand across his forehead, massaging temples that felt as if they had been constantly throbbing for days.

The pressure of work was enormous. Running the principality as well as his own business interests meant there wasn't a spare minute in the day. Rising at first light, he started the day with a five-mile run, ending it with a punishing session in the gym, desperately trying to ease the knots in his muscles, persuade his brain to switch off and let him sleep. Which rarely happened.

He slid his hand across his closed lids, pinching the bridge of his nose. He had always thought he thrived on pressure. On pushing himself harder and harder. It was what he did. So why was there no sense of satisfaction? Just hollowness inside. He was back in Ravenino, doing the job he'd thought he'd always wanted, albeit only as a proxy. He had fully expected to be hit by any one of a number of negative emotions that had to be lying in wait for him on his return to his homeland. Resentment, hostility, envy.

What he had never expected to feel was… nothing. Not then, when he had first set foot on Ravenino soil. And not now, three weeks in, when his authoritative command had steered the principality away from the brink of uncertainty, calmed the financial markets and reassured the investors. He was doing a good job, he knew that. He would leave the principality in a better shape than he'd found it. Whenever that was.

He leaned back in his chair, stretching out his spine. Yesterday they'd had good news. Taddeo had been brought out of his coma, and all the signs were that he would make a full recovery. It would just take time. Leo thought back to Cordelia's face when she had come in to tell him. Not just shining with relief but love too. She had clearly married the right brother after all. Leo gazed out of the window. Funny how things turned out.

Immediately his mind conjured up an image of Emma, the way it always did when he stopped working for as much as a second. Which was a good reason not to stop. Because he didn't want to be reminded of her—not when his last memory was of the hurt on her face before she had turned away. Anguish. Sorrow. All inflicted by him.

Since then a few brief phone calls had done nothing to repair the damage. Polite enquiries about one another's health, updates on Taddeo's progress, Emma's voice noticeably devoid of emotion, even when he had asked her about the scan. All was fine apparently. That was all he could get out of her. It was like a light had gone out. She never asked when he might be coming home. Perhaps she didn't care. Perhaps she was glad to see the back of him. He wouldn't have blamed her.

But he'd had to be firm. He didn't want Emma here in Ravenino. But neither did he want to examine the reasons too deeply. This place, the land that he had once loved so much, that he would have devoted his life to, given his life *for* if necessary, in a heartbeat, had become his nemesis.

He turned to look out of the window, where the principality was laid out before him. Tree-covered hills, clusters of houses, a sparkling sea, all representing nothing but failure. His failure to be the right son, the true heir. His failure to be the man he had always thought he was.

Was that why he couldn't bear to bring Emma here? He tried to push the thought away, but it refused to budge. Was it because he couldn't bear the idea of her witnessing his failings that he was so determined to keep her away? Because he didn't want her to see him for the man he really was? Because her opinion of him mattered. She mattered. Too much. In fact, the jolt of realisation hit him square between the eyes.

Emma was the only thing in his life that mattered at all.

The phone on the desk rang and with some relief Leo reached forward to answer it. The work might be all-consuming, but it was also his friend. It kept the demons at bay.

The thud of her heart sounded in her ears as Emma's first sighting of the principality of Ravenino came into view.

Jagged cliffs covered in dense green-ery fell to a turquoise sea dotted with small white boats. Hundreds of pastel-coloured houses clung to the vertiginous rocks, white sandy coves fringed the shore. And then, as the aeroplane banked, ready to land, there it was—the magnificent Castello Ravenino, perched right on the water's edge, grand and proud, a symbol of power and rule, of centuries of history.

Pulling her bag down from the overhead locker, Emma joined the queue to exit the plane, her fellow passengers chattering noisily as if just arriving here was cause for celebration in itself. Holidaymakers or residents, or probably a mixture of both, they eagerly stepped onto the tarmac, dragging their suitcases, holding on to the hands of their children, hurrying towards passport control.

But Emma could find no such cause for celebration. Far from it. Only nerves, batting inside her like the wings of a bird, a mouth so dry she feared she might never be able to speak again.

But somehow the taxi driver understood her instructions to take her to the Castello and now, as she stared up at the imposing stone walls, she knew there was no going back.

Her decision to come to Ravenino had been made in the middle of another sleepless night. Another night when Leo had dominated her thoughts, stealing into her dreams, waking her with his hands squeezed around her heart. Standing under the shower one morning, she had started to formulate her plan. She couldn't carry on like this. She couldn't pretend any more. She wasn't prepared to live this sort of half-life any longer. His wife in name, but with no power, no role. His lover when it suited him, but only ever on his terms, at his command. Which meant she only had one option. She had to confront Leo and tell the truth.

Taddeo's accident had only highlighted the dire state of their relationship. At a time of crisis, when most couples turned to their partners for help and support, Leo had pushed her away. Totally shut her out. Cruelly rebuffed her.

Emma understood how hard returning to Ravenino was for him, even if he had refused to show her any emotion. Despite his cool demeanour, she had seen it in the taut lines of his face, heard it in the gravel of his voice. In retrospect, that should have been enough to warn her off but, no, she had jumped in with both feet, suggesting she go with him, driven by an innocent desire to ease his burden. No, not just that. In truth she had been driven by a desperate need to prove that she meant something to him.

Fool that she was.

The cold look he had given her was etched for ever on her mind. His cruel words were still ringing in her head: *'the encumbrance of a pregnant wife tagging along.'* It was all there in those damning words. Their whole relationship encapsulated in a few bitter words. If she had worried she meant nothing to him, she'd been wrong. She did mean something to him—nuisance, burden, responsibility. A thorn in his side. And one he was stuck with for ever.

Well, not any more. If it suited Leo to pretend that she had no feelings, or he was just too damned selfish to care if she did, she was going to put him straight. Because Emma was beset with a whole surge of feelings, tormenting her day and night. Stealing her sleep, her appetite, the glow from her cheeks and the light in her eyes. Stealing her dignity and her self-respect.

These past few weeks she had barely been able to look at herself in the mirror, repelled by the face that stared back at her. The face of someone too weak, too feeble to stand up for herself. Who had allowed herself to be used by a man who cared nothing for her.

Who pined for a man in his absence when his presence only gave her pain. Worse, far worse, to fall in love with this man. Because, yes, Emma had had to face up to that torturous fact too. Only by doing so would she ever be able to move on.

Which was why she was here. This was it. Do or die. She was going to tell him how she felt about him. *Really felt.* And if that was like signing her own death warrant, then so be it. Because maybe a quick, clean kill would be easier in the end. Put her out of her misery. Anything had to be better than being eaten away by the agonising torture of staying silent, hiding her true emotions, pretending she didn't love him…

Walking up the long flight of steps, she felt her heart grow heavier with every tread. Her hand trembled as she reached for the bronze bell button, hearing it echo inside, the sound of a dog barking. Hunching her shoulders, she waited, half expecting a colony of bats to appear, flapping around her head to warn her off.

But there were no bats, just a polite butler who enquired her name, registering no hint of surprise when she had announced herself as Signora Ravenino. Escorting her into the cavernous hallway, Emma gazed around at the sweeping stone staircase, the polished marble floor, the heavy brass chandeliers. So this was where Leo had grown up, the place he had thought would always be home. A lump formed in her throat. For Leo's loss. For her own loss. Feelings, she told herself sternly. Just more feelings.

Beside her the butler was trying to usher her into a salon, telling her he would inform Signor Ravenino of her arrival. But Emma stood firm. She didn't want Leo to have any advance warning that she was here. Surprise was the only weapon she had in her armoury. It was why she hadn't told him she was coming. A skilled negotiator when it suited him, she didn't want to give him time to prepare his reaction. This exchange had to be raw, real. That was the whole point. She had to look into his eyes when she told him the truth. She had to see what was really there. No matter how painful that might be.

Pasting on the most winning expression she could muster, she explained to the butler that her visit was a surprise. That she would like to arrive unannounced. After a moment's hesitation he informed her that the Signor was working in the library and that if she would like to follow him, he would show her the way. A flight of stairs led them along a dark corridor until they finally stopped outside an enormous pair of panelled oak doors.

With a small bow the butler left her. Taking in a huge breath, the bravest breath of her life, Emma grasped the twin handles and pushed.

'Not now.' Leo didn't look up from his paperwork. The day had been beset with problems and he didn't need anyone coming in with any more. What he needed was to be left in peace.

The faint sound of a breath stilled his hand, locking his muscles in place. *No. It couldn't be.* Very slowly he lifted his head.

'Hello, Leo.'

A smack of shock hit him between the eyes. *Emma!* He swallowed hard. But still the shock reverberated through him, thrumming in his blood. Something almost like panic set in. This reaction was too extreme—he had to take measures to control it.

'What are you doing here?' He made no attempt at courtesy, cursing the thud of his heart, the fact she looked so small and slight standing in the doorway. The way it pulled at something inside him.

'I had to come and see you.'

'The baby?' With of jolt of horror he jumped to his feet. 'Something is wrong?'

'No, Leo, the baby is fine.'

Relief washed over him but still the pounding of his heart refused to be tamed.

'Then what?' His hands gripped the edge of the desk. 'What is so urgent that you couldn't tell me over the phone?'

'What I have to say needs to be said face to face.'

Leo's mind raced with possibilities, none of them good. His brows drew into a scowl.

Emma advanced into the room, the anguished determination written all over her pale face punching him low in the gut.

She stopped six feet away from where Leo still stood behind his desk, unable to move. Scarcely able to breathe. 'I have to tell you…' She paused, then swallowed. 'That I can't carry on with our relationship. Not as it stands at present.'

Leo stilled, ice flooding through his veins. What nonsense was this? He drew in a steadying breath, searching for the measured response that had to be there somewhere.

'If you mean because I have to be here in Ravenino, then frankly, Emma, I would have expected more understanding from you.' He firmed his lips. 'This situation is not of my making. I didn't *ask* my brother to fall off a horse. I didn't *ask* to take over the ruling of the principality. But these events have happened and now I am left to deal with them.'

'I'm not talking about your being here in Ravenino.' Slowly she took another couple of steps towards him, her voice low, her eyes too bright. 'I'm talking about our relationship as a whole. All of it. Me and you, man and wife. It's not working.'

He heard the curse fall from his lips and, turning his back, made himself count several beats before facing her again.

'Emma.' His voice was laced with warning. 'I refuse to play these stupid games.'

The slight shake of her head did nothing to tame his blood.

'Of course you will carry on with our relationship. We are man and wife. And that's an end to it.'

But her infuriating silence suggested otherwise, more inflammatory than any words.

Something inside Leo leapt and growled. Anger? Alarm? Or fear?

'I don't have time for this.' His voice grew harsher. 'Whatever your problem is, it will have to wait. There are far more pressing issues I need to deal with.'

'No, Leo. It won't wait.' When she finally spoke, he could hear the defiance, see its shimmer in her slender frame. Two more steps and she was on the other side of his desk, her shoulders back, her head high. She was holding on to her composure, but her gaze was wild, tearing into Leo, producing a surge of emotion he couldn't even put a name to. 'This needs to be said now and I am going to say it.'

'Very well.' Leo forced his clenched jaw to unlock enough to say a few words. To affect an air of indifference. 'If you must.'

He heard her take a breath, saw the way it swelled her breasts beneath the loose-fitting silk blouse.

'When I entered into this marriage I thought I could deal with it the same way as you. Purely as a deal to secure the future of our unborn child. I thought I could cope with that. That the security you were offering would make up for the lack of…of emotional attachment. But now I find that it doesn't. And that changes everything. Now I find I have to be honest, both with myself and with you. And I need you to be honest in return.'

'I have never been anything but honest, Emma.' Impatience clawed at his voice.

'Then perhaps I am at fault for looking for something that isn't there.' Her hands fluttered to her abdomen, smoothing over the slight swell beneath the blue fabric before letting her hands rest there, possessively, protectively. As if she needed to guard their unborn child from him. 'And that is the problem I have to address. The reason I am here.

'I can't carry on the way we are any longer. I can't pretend that I am fine with your brisk efficiency, your lack of emotion. The way you would come to my bed but then sneak away before morning, as if what we had just done was wrong, sordid. You made me feel used, ashamed. You have taken the intimacy between us, something precious, special, at least to me, and turned it into something dirty. Shameful.'

'That was never my intention...'

'And then when you were called here to Ravenino, the place that means so much to you, you pushed me away again. Shut me out.'

Leo dragged a hand through his hair. Why was she persisting in raking over this when no good would come of it?

'You erected barriers right from the start, enforced boundaries to keep me out. To keep me in my place. And it worked for a while. I thought I could stick to the rules. But now I find I can't. It's too hard.'

Holding himself totally still, Leo's mind whirred to find ways to put an end to this misery. If Emma was unhappy, and clearly she was, he would renegotiate the terms, strike another deal. This was what he did. What he was good at. Even if right now it felt as if a heavy boot was pressing down on his chest. He just had to fight harder to maintain control. He had no choice.

'And what exactly is it that you find so hard?' He used sarcasm to mask his growing agitation.

But then Emma's lip trembled, taunting him, driving him nearly mad.

'Everything.' Her shuddering sigh racked her whole body. 'I know the last thing you wanted was to have our marriage complicated by messy emotions. And I'm sorry for that. Truly I am. But I can't help it.'

'Can't help what?'

'I can't help being in love with you.'

The words bloomed inside his head, spreading hot and thick, pounding through him.

Emma was in love with him? How was that possible?

He had worked so hard not to let their relationship fall into this trap. Keeping himself emotionally sterile at all times. It had never been a problem before. Distancing himself from the many women that had graced his bed in recent years had been easy. Impervious to their simpering flattery or declarations of ardour, his heart had been left completely untouched. It only went to prove what he had known all along. He wasn't capable of love. His mother's betrayal had killed his heart stone dead.

But with Emma it was different. Somehow, she had managed to creep beneath his impregnable defences. So he had redoubled his efforts to keep her at bay, cutting short the time they spent together, working even longer hours than were absolutely necessary, dragging himself from her bed when all he wanted to do was pull her into his arms, feel her skin against his as they drifted off to sleep, wake to see her head next to him on the pillow. Even though every night tearing himself away from her was more difficult than the one before.

But he had done it. He had been strong, for Emma's sake. And he'd thought he had succeeded. That his effort hadn't been in vain. Until now. Until this.

He could feel Emma's eyes locked on his face, tracking every twitch of muscle, seeking out the turmoil that lay just beneath the surface. Well, she would not find it. He refused to expose his emotions to her. He had no intention of laying his feelings bare. He didn't even understand them himself, except to know they were raw and powerful and pulled his skin too tight. No, this situation needed to be calmed and contained, and the sooner the better. Before things got completely out of hand.

He twisted away, taking a second to compose himself, to steady the pounding of his blood. Turning back on a sharp intake of breath, he was ready to face her again.

'I agree this is an unfortunate situation.' But not her eyes. He couldn't look into those pale blue eyes for fear of coming undone. Instead his gaze hovered somewhere over the top of her head. 'But perhaps you are mistaken.'

'I am not mistaken, Leo.'

'Is it possible the pregnancy is confusing your emotions?'

'Don't, Leo.' She flashed him a murderous look. 'Just don't.'

'Mi dispiace?'

'Please don't patronise me by suggesting I can't interpret my own feelings. At least do me the courtesy of acknowledging that what I say is the truth. My truth. I have been in love with you for weeks, months, maybe since the first time we met. Those are the facts.'

'And what am I supposed to do with these facts?' The twist in his gut turned to anger, something he could deal with. 'You turn up here uninvited, unannounced, making wild announcements about not being able to carry on with our relationship. How exactly do you expect me to react?'

'I just want honesty, Leo, that's all. The same honesty as I have shown to you.'

'Very well.' He ground down on his jaw. 'You need to know that I will not be blackmailed.'

'Blackmailed?' The bitter word turned to astonishment on her open lips.

'Yes, blackmailed, Emma. In my experience, the only reason a woman tells a man she loves him is to goad him into responding. Because she wants to hear the words back. Because that gives her power.'

A look of disgust crossed Emma's face. Bizarrely this brought relief. Disgust he could cope with. It was so much easier to deal with than the sight of Emma hurting.

'I suspect you have had too much time on your hands. Perhaps you have found these last few weeks at Villa Magenta rather boring. Your charity work not enough to occupy you. The novelty of having your every need catered for, every comfort at your disposal wearing off so you have looked around to find something to account for your dissatisfaction. And that something was me.

'But I will not be blackmailed, Emma. By you or anyone else. I will not be tricked into sharing sentiments I don't feel, just to make you feel better.'

He paused, the weight of his words swinging like lead between them. Up until now he had managed to avoid the full glare of her eyes, his gaze flitting lightly over her face, knowing there was no safe place to land. But he could avoid them no longer. He had to deal with whatever horror he saw. Because deal with it he would. Quickly and efficiently. A clean kill. It was kinder in the end.

Her silence was total, not as much as a breath stirring the air. But the eyes he finally met were wide, unblinking. And dry. Bone dry. Dead.

Tears he had been expecting. He could have dealt with them. Many a woman had tried to use them as a weapon against him when things hadn't been going their way, only to find they'd left him completely unmoved. But Emma's steady stare tore him apart.

'You have nothing further to say?' Leo could stand this cruel silence no longer. He had to bring it to an end.

'No.' She shook her head, her fingers finding a lock of hair over her shoulder, smoothing it down. 'I came here looking for honesty to try and make sense of our relationship and find a way forward. And you have given me that honesty. For which I thank you.'

She was thanking him? For being a cold-hearted brute?

'I will leave you in peace now. I have arrangements to make.'

'What arrangements?' His voice growled with suspicion.

'I am going to go back to the UK. I need some time to sort out my head.'

'You will do no such thing.'

'I don't need your permission, Leo. I am your wife, not your possession.'

'And as my wife I order you to stay here.'

'Here, as in Ravenino? The place you were so determined I should never even visit?'

'Here, as in Italy. You will return to Villa Magenta.'

'And what will you do? Have Luigi follow me around again, making sure I don't escape?'

'I will put my entire security team onto it if necessary.' Frustration clawed at his throat. *How had it come to this?* 'You are not only my wife but you are carrying my child. I absolutely forbid your returning to England.'

'You can't stop me, Leo.' She tightened her jaw. 'Unless you intend to physically restrain me, of course. No doubt there is a dungeon around here somewhere you could throw me into.'

Leo seethed with impotent rage. *There was.* And he *was* tempted.

'So what exactly do you intend to do in England? Go back to your family and their squalid little encampment in a muddy field? Start making daisy chains for a living?'

'No.'

'Have that delightful mother of yours tell you what a miserable failure you are?' He was building up a head of steam now, a rush of white noise in his ears. 'Do you think she will welcome you back, Emma? Or will she be locking away her latest boyfriend for fear you might get your claws into him?'

The flinch of pain that marred Emma's beautiful face slashed into his soul, hard and deep. But panic drove him on. He would not lose her. He could not lose her.

'And don't think for one moment I will let that toxic woman anywhere near my child. I expressly forbid any contact with her. Ever.'

His frantic gaze ran over her body, alive to every small movement. As if she might vanish before his eyes.

'I will return to London.' The struggle to hold on to her composure cracked in her voice.

'To live where, exactly?'

'I don't know, Leo.' A dreadful weariness weighted her words. 'But I will find somewhere. I have done it before.'

'For how long?'

'Two or three months? I need some headspace, time to think things through.'

'Very well.' He raked a hand through his hair. He had to assume some sort of control if he was to get through this. 'But I have two conditions. Firstly, I will be the one to arrange accommodation for you in London. And secondly, you will return to Italy before the baby is born.'

Emma's pause was mercifully short before she gave a brief nod.

'I have your word?'

'Yes, Leo, you have my word.'

'Because if not…'

'I *said* you have my word.'

Leo allowed himself to breathe.

'In that case I will have the jet put on standby for you. The flight will go via Milan so you can collect your belongings from Villa Magenta.'

He moved back behind the desk, his eyes

cast down, his hands shuffling the papers he no longer gave a damn about.

'I will be in touch in due course.'

He waited for sounds of movement, for Emma to leave, slamming the doors behind her. Or stay…coming towards him to affect some sort of reconciliation. To tell him that she had overreacted. To beat her fists against his chest. To scream at him what a bastard he was. But hearing nothing he flicked his eyes upwards to find her still standing there, her hands clasped under the slight swell of her bump, wide eyes staring at him from beneath that fringe.

Leo swallowed. Goddamn the woman.

'I will say goodbye, then.' Her voice was very small.

'Goodbye, Emma.' He looked back down at the paperwork.

'Oh, one more thing.' With some effort he raised his head again. When was she going to be done torturing him?

'When I had the scan…they asked if I wanted to know the baby's sex.'

'And…?' Leo felt his heart rate spike dramatically.

'I said yes.' Emma held his gaze, strong and blue. 'It's a boy, Leo. You are going to have a son.'

CHAPTER TWELVE

EMMA WAITED FOR the pain to kick in, almost welcoming it. Because anything had to be better than this frozen inertia. Like she had been drugged. Anaesthetised. She knew the agony was there, that Leo's cruel words had ripped her wide open, his reaction more brutal, more merciless than her worst fears. But she couldn't feel the wounds. Yet. Maybe her poor body was refusing to process them.

But at least she had managed to stand upright in front of Leo. She hadn't collapsed in a heap of misery. She had remained coherent, conducting herself with decorum in the face of more heartbreak than she had ever thought possible. At least she had walked out of that library with her head held high. Even if she had no idea how she'd done it.

But now the corridor seemed to be closing in on her, the musty smell of the books in the library lingering in her nostrils suddenly making her feel nauseous. She felt for the wall to steady herself. The dimensions of the space seemed to be changing, surging and retreating. Someone was coming towards her, a tall slight figure, gliding rather than walking, surrounded by white light. Emma half closed her eyes.

'Dio mio!' The figure had her arm around her shoulders now. Bony but warm, flesh and blood. So she was real, not an apparition. 'Emma? It is Emma, isn't it?'

Emma nodded weakly, letting her head rest against the woman's shoulder.

'Here, let me help you to a chair.'

A couple of staggering steps took them to a nearby seat.

'I should send for a doctor?' The woman crouched down beside her, taking Emma's hand in hers.

'No.' Emma tried to shake her head but it felt as if her brain was loose inside. 'No, I'll be fine in a minute.'

'Is it the baby?'

'No.' How did this person know she was pregnant? 'Well, it does make me feel a bit dizzy sometimes.' It was such an effort to talk. 'But, really, it will pass.'

'Then wait here. I will fetch Leonardo.'

'No!' The vehemence in Emma's voice

sent a look of surprise across this woman's face. She was very beautiful, Emma realised as her senses started to return. Fine-boned, wide dark eyes searched her face. *Cordelia*. Of course, it had to be. 'Please don't tell him.'

'Well, if you are sure?' She stood up, her puzzled gaze travelling down the corridor until a member of staff appeared, as if she had conjured him up by thought alone. Rapid instructions were issued before she turned back to Emma. 'Are you well enough to move into the salon?'

'Yes, I think so.' Emma struggled to her feet to prove a strength she was far from feeling. Sandwiched between Cordelia and the servant she was guided into a grand salon and gently lowered onto a gilded sofa.

'Giovanni will bring you some water. Is there anything else you need?'

'No, I will be fine now, thank you.'

'Would you like me to stay with you? I was on my way to visit my husband in hospital but…'

'No, really, you go.'

She had reached the door before she turned to look back at Emma with an apologetic smile. 'Forgive me, I didn't even introduce myself. I am Cordelia. Your sister-in-law.'

'How do you do?' Emma gave her a faint

smile. 'And thank you for looking after me. You must think me very feeble.'

'On the contrary…' Cordelia's dark eyes swept over her. 'You are married to Leonardo. That in itself takes strength and courage. He would never choose a wife who didn't possess such qualities.'

Emma looked down, swallowing hard.

'I appreciate that coming back to Ravenino has been very hard for him. Frankly his mood has been quite black. Which is why I am so pleased to see you. I'm sure having you here will be a great comfort to him.'

'I doubt that.'

'Don't underestimate yourself, Emma. He has missed you a great deal.'

'He…he said that?'

'Not exactly.' Cordelia adjusted the handbag over the crook of her arm. 'Leonardo is not a man to voice his emotions. But you forget that I know him. And I know when a woman has finally won his heart. Congratulations, Emma, I hope you will both be very happy.'

Stepping out onto the balcony, Emma took a lungful of fresh air. Having been fussed over by various members of staff for the past hour, she desperately craved solitude, time to think.

The view, at least, was calming. Sea and sky stretching in all directions, the shape of the mainland just visible on the horizon. A fishing boat headed towards the harbour, excited seagulls squawking in its wake. Everything about this place was so steeped in history and tradition you could feel it in the very air you breathed. A living history that Leo had been written out of.

Emma bit down on the tremble of her lip. How many times must he have stood gazing at this view? How many times must he have visited his beloved Ravenino in his head? And what must it feel like to be back here now? To have everything he had lost tantalisingly placed back in his hands, but only for a short while. Just long enough to rub salt into the wounds.

Leo's treatment of her couldn't have been more brutal. But beneath the cruel words, the arrogant authority, had she caught a glimpse of something else? Something that looked like torment. Like he was being pulled in two directions. Like being here was ripping him apart.

Cordelia's voice sounded in her head. *'He has missed you a great deal.'* Was that possible? *'I know when a woman has finally won his heart.'* She was wrong, she had to be. But her words had been enough to make Emma pause. To cancel the flight that had been put on standby for her, at least for today. Because running away no longer seemed like the answer. Staying and fighting did. Fighting for what she believed in. For happiness that could only be found in Leo's arms, in his bed, in his heart... Fighting for the man that she loved.

Her first thought had been to flee. To put some space between her and Leo in the desperate hope that if she returned to the UK, she might be able to patch up her broken heart enough to come back stronger in time for the birth. But the rules would have to change. She would be adamant about that. She would insist that she and the baby have their own apartment. Live separate lives. Leo could have unrestricted access to their child, but that's all. She couldn't go back to the arrangement they had shared at Villa Magenta. It was too painful. Too degrading.

Her head had told her this was the only way forward. But her heart refused to agree, twisting inside her now, telling her to fight for what she wanted, goading her into action. Condemning herself to such a cold, sterile existence would never make her happy. She would be existing rather than thriving, trapped in the twilight of a half-life where the sun would never shine. Living alongside the man she loved but who could never be hers. Who only ever came to her in her dreams.

Strength and courage. Did she possess enough of those qualities to try one more time? One last attempt to get inside Leo's head, to break through the protective wall and expose the turmoil that lay beneath. Because she was pretty sure that what was inside was broken, hurting. And despite everything, she knew she wanted to help him. To heal him. Even if it turned out to be her parting gift.

A strange sensation fluttered in her stomach and Emma grasped the stone balustrade. She hoped she wasn't going to feel faint again. But no. She spread her hands over her belly, waiting. There it was again. The baby. Their baby. Moving inside her, like it was trying to tell her something. Too gentle to be called a kick, yet more powerful than the mightiest blow. Emma closed her eyes against the swell of emotion. Here was the strength she needed. Now all she had to do was use it.

The cobbled streets of Ravenino greeted Leo like an old friend, twisting and turning their way down narrow alleys, opening up into ancient piazzas, ascending long flights of steps to white-painted churches. Leo knew every inch of the place. It was written into his DNA. As kids, he and Taddeo had treated the town like their playground, taking every opportunity to escape the walls of the Castello in search of freedom.

With Leo the brains of the operation and Taddeo egging him on, they had often been found stripped half-naked splashing in a fountain when they should have been in lessons, riding a donkey through the town with the Castello security team in hot pursuit. There had been punishments, of course. Harsh physical punishments, largely taken by Leo, the elder brother. The one who should have known better. But he hadn't minded. Taller and stronger than Taddeo, it was only right he'd taken the brunt of it. Besides, he'd loved his brother. He would have done anything for him.

But as the years had gone on their relationship had changed, responsibility settling on Leo's shoulders, seeing him start to obey the rules, take his lessons seriously, frequently travelling abroad for months at a time to further his education. Taddeo, meanwhile, had discovered women, lots of women. And partying. Frequently crashing home drunk when Leo had already been behind his desk, preparing for another day of dry instruction.

Words had been exchanged. Leo informing his brother it was time he grew up, Taddeo demanding to know when Leo had turned into such a crashing bore.

By the time their father died they had become very different people. But the shock of finding out he was to be the next Conte had hit Taddeo almost as hard as Leo. Neither of them had handled it well, and Taddeo's arrogant assumption that Leo would take on much of the responsibility behind the scenes, effectively leaving him to carry on with his hedonistic lifestyle, had sent Leo into a storm of fury. Tempers had flared, voices had been raised. And when Taddeo had got wind that Leo had tried to honour his pledge to Cordelia and she had turned him down, he had used that to full advantage to get under Leo's skin. To taunt him in a way that only siblings could. And that, for Leo, had been the final straw. He'd wanted nothing more to do with Ravenino. Nothing more to do with Taddeo.

Turning the corner, he found himself in front of the town hall, the clock just starting to strike the hour. On either side of the dial, bronze figures took aim at the bell beneath, swinging their hammers with never diminishing strength.

'You and me, Leo,' Taddeo had once said,

gazing up as he had linked his skinny arm through his brother's. 'One day we will be strong, just like them.'

But were they? Not Taddeo, incapacitated by an accident, lying in a hospital bed. And Leo himself? Sometimes it felt as if the stronger he was determined to be, the weaker he became. Certainly as far as Emma was concerned.

Emma. The memory of her standing there in the library, so upright, so proud, cut through him like a blade. But she shouldn't have come here. And she certainly shouldn't have declared her love for him.

He turned away, retracing his steps to the Castello. Being summoned to Ravenino had been a cruel blow, but Leo had counted on there being *one* positive outcome. Being away from Emma would give him time to clear his head, order his thoughts. But that hadn't happened. Emma was permanently there—no matter where he was, what he was doing. A receptor in his brain, a tug in his gut, a pulse in his groin. He carried her with him wherever he went. Sometimes it felt as if she was attacking him on all fronts, just by existing. Just by being Emma.

Which was why his reaction had been so hostile when she had turned up this afternoon, out of the blue, talking about love. She was disobeying his orders. She was breaking the rules. She was messing with his head. She had even found out the sex of their baby without his permission.

A boy! His son! Pride reared up inside him again, constricting his throat. A daughter would have been just as joyous, but he couldn't help the way the thought of a son puffed out his chest, called to him on some primal level. And the fact that Emma had discovered it first no longer mattered one jot.

Inside the Castello grounds now, Leo gazed up at the imposing fortress, the granite walls, the towering turrets. A symbol of strength and power through the centuries, it epitomised everything he'd thought he'd stood for. Everything he had thought he'd wanted. And yet now…now he realised he had been mistaken. By coming back to the principality, he had been forced to face his nemesis, only to find it was no such thing. Ravenino was his past, not his future. It was not preventing him from moving on. He alone was doing that.

It was a shocking revelation. Leo looked around him, breathing deeply, searching for the emotion that had to be there. Testing himself. Almost willing himself to feel what he had told himself he had to feel. Loss, regret, anger, bitterness. Because to deny it was to make a mockery of the last three years of his life. Years when he had skated over the surface of his life. Never standing still enough to examine the motives behind his behaviour. Never stopping to look at what lay beneath for fear it would be too hard.

But Emma had challenged him right from the start. From the moment she had put her slender fingers on the keyboard and composed that article. From the flash of her eyes that night in London, the shock revelation she was pregnant, the torment of trying to live alongside her at Villa Magenta.

And now this. By declaring her love for him. Always inside his head. Always Emma.

He started walking again, his feet taking him around the side of the Castello, towards the family chapel and the graveyard that was the final resting place for generations of Raveninos. He followed the grassy path that led to his mother's grave, set against the wall, catching the quiet rays of the afternoon sun. He had been here many times over the years, Taddeo by his side, placing flowers in the vase beneath the headstone, paying their respects to their mother who had died before her time. But now there was another grave, a newer headstone.

Alberto Leonardo Ravenino
May he rest in peace

A simple inscription sharply carved into the black granite.

Leo squatted down beside the grave. He now regretted refusing to attend Alberto's funeral. Regretted not having been there to pay his last respects to the man who had raised him. The man who Leo had thought to be his father for twenty-eight years. At the time he had been too consumed with rage to think straight. He had hated Alberto for being so weak—for daring to love a woman who had betrayed him in the worst possible way. For keeping the lie to himself until the very last moment. Leo had raged against the selfishness of his final act—casting him aside, just to ease his own conscience.

Now that anger had gone, replaced with understanding, sympathy even. He truly hoped Alberto was at peace. As a ray of sunlight flickered from one grave to the other, he realised he even wished the same for his mother. That they had found eternal happiness together, if ever such a thing were to be found.

Whatever had happened to him?

Emma. That was what. Emma had changed

his whole perspective on life. Changed his priorities. Made him come alive. Made him feel. Not the shallow emotions shown to the faceless women who had shared his bed. Not the hatred and bitterness that he had harboured for so long. Nurtured even. Afraid that if he let go of it there would be nothing left of him. That his antipathy had made him the man he was.

With a rush of adrenaline his mind cleared. His fractured thoughts finally shaped into a clear picture.

Emma was his tormentor and his liberator. The light to his dark. She was everything to him. And yet he had sent her away...

Rising to his feet, Leo pushed back shoulders that were locked with tension. Cowardice, denial, stupidity, he could think of a host of reasons for his behaviour. But none that excused it. Because the truth was he had panicked.

Emma's brave, beautiful, astonishing words had shaken the world beneath his feet. She had forced him to face the unthinkable. Not the knowledge she had fallen in love with him. That truth he held against his heart like the most precious jewel, warm and safe. Nothing and no one would take that away from him.

But the way her confession had flayed him, laying him bare, ripping him open for all to see. Showing him he was not the man he had told himself he was—clinical, unemotional, controlled. Making him feel what he told himself he could not feel. Did not want to feel. *And yet he did.* More deeply, more passionately than he could ever have imagined. *Love.* So powerful it hurt. So strong it burned. *He loved Emma.* That was an absolute, indisputable fact. One that he had realised the second Emma had made her confession. One that he had most probably always known but had stubbornly refused to acknowledge.

And so he had gone on the attack. Fought back. Because when you were exposed, that's what you did. When the outer layers had been stripped away, leaving you nowhere to hide, what other choice did you have?

But of course there were other choices. Honesty, for example. Sincerity, truth. Things that he had prided himself on. Things he would have said he stood for, until now. Until Emma had exposed him as a charlatan.

He had to explain—right away! He had to take her in his arms, hold her, feel her, inhale her. Make her a part of him. Never let her go. *But first he had to find her.*

Furiously cursing himself for ever sending

her away, he set off between the gravestones at a rapid pace, small birds taking flight as he disturbed their peace. But then reality kicked in and he stopped. Emma had gone. She would be in Milan by now, maybe back at Villa Magenta, packing her bags. He glared at his watch as if he could halt time. He needed to get the jet back here as fast as possible to take him to Emma before she instructed the pilot to fly her to London.

He tugged his phone out of his pocket, frantically making the call, holding the phone to his ear, scuffing the earth at his feet. *Come on, come on.*

'Leo.'

Emma. His Emma.

It took a second for him to realise the voice—*her voice*—had not come over the phone.

His head jerked up, his heart thudding in his ears. Standing about ten feet away she was framed between two gravestones, motionless, but so very alive amongst his sleeping relatives. Warm flesh and soft lips and a heart bigger than any he had ever known. And if that wasn't enough, if that wasn't far more than he ever deserved, she was carrying his child. His son. The next generation. Not the next Conte di Ravenino, he didn't give a damn about that any more, but something far more precious. His own family. *His own future*. *Dio*, what a fool he had been. A huge surge of emotion flooded through him, a tidal wave more powerful than anything he had ever felt before.

'Emma.' He couldn't keep the tremor from his voice. 'You...you came back.'

'I never left, Leo.' She twisted her hands in front of her. 'I couldn't.'

'Emma... I...'

'No, let me speak.' Determination lifted her chin, fixing her gaze on his. *Dio*, he loved her so much. 'I know you don't want me here, that you thought I had gone...'

'No... I...' He started towards her, but she took a step back, holding her hands out before her as if to ward him off.

'But I couldn't leave before trying one last time...'

'No, you don't understand. You don't need to try anything. You don't need to do anything.'

'Oh, but I do, Leo.' She gave a small shake of the head. 'Because I will never forgive myself, never find peace if I don't give you the opportunity, one last time, to tell me what you feel in your heart. About me. About us.'

'Oh, Emma.' His voice choked, Leo tried to

close the space between them, but for every step he took forward, she took one back, stumbling over the long grass at the side of the pathway. *'Attenta!'* He stretched out a hand but dared come no closer. 'Please, be careful.'

'I'm fine.' She steadied herself, pushing back her shoulders, taking in a gasp of breath.

But she wasn't fine. She was fragile, sensitive, delicate. Flesh and blood. Skin and bones. And yet still she'd found the strength to confront him. Because she was also brave. The bravest person he had ever known. And for some unknown reason this perfect woman, this woman so beautiful, both inside and out, loved him.

He wasn't worthy. The thought struck him like a blow. He would never be worthy of such a woman. Doubts crowded in, drawing down his brows into a scowl. And Emma noticed, biting down on her lip to stop the tremble. But still she pressed on.

'So I am going to ask you this, Leo. And I will accept your answer with all its implications.' Her chest rose on a brave breath. 'Do you think there is any chance that you could ever find it in your heart to love me?'

Oh, Emma. Darling Emma.

'More than a chance.' He felt the swell of

love crowding his chest, filling his lungs. 'A certainty.'

Emma stared at him, that soft mouth opening in surprise. 'A...a certainty?'

'*Sì.*' Leo struggled to find the words trapped so deeply inside him. 'Because I already love you, Emma. In fact, I think I always have.'

They were the right words but the wrong tone, the struggle to stop his voice from cracking making them sound harsh, unfeeling.

Uncertainty flickered in Emma's eyes. 'Please don't say that if it isn't true, Leo.' Her hands strayed to the swell of her belly. 'I only want the truth.'

'Then hear this as the truth. *Ti amo.* I love you, Emma.'

He wanted to take her in his arms, to crush her against his chest. He wanted to kiss her, fiercely, with everything he had. He wanted to show his love in a way that words could never do. But he knew he had to be cautious.

One step at a time he stole the space between them, holding Emma still with his eyes, scared that one wrong move, one wrong word might see her bolt like a startled horse. Because she still looked totally stunned. Disbelieving.

Finally, she was in his arms. But her posture was stiff, her arms down by her sides. Her eyes, when he caught her chin to raise them to his, wide and blue as the sky.

'I love you, Emma.' He repeated the words, a soft whisper of breath against her face. 'With all that I have, all that I am.'

'Leo… I…'

'Hear it in my voice. See it in my eyes. And if that's not enough…' He reached for her hand, so small, chilled, despite the warmth of the late afternoon, and raised it to his chest. 'Feel it in my heart and know that it is true.'

'Oh, Leo.' Eyes shining, she raised her face to his gaze, and Leo could only stare in wonder at the woman he loved so much. The upturn of her nose, the fine cheekbones, the line of her closed lips. He loved every inch of her. Every single molecule that made her who she was. He squeezed the hand against his chest, warming it, willing her to feel the thud of his heart. But to his dismay tears had started to spill from her eyes, silently rolling down her cheeks, a flood of them.

He had never seen her cry before. Not once. Not after everything he had put her through. As his fingertips touched the dampness of her tears his heart splintered into a thousand pieces.

'Don't cry, Emma. Please.' He fell to his knees, down in the dirt where he belonged. Wrapping his arms around her waist he buried his face in her belly. 'I know I have treated you very badly, that I don't deserve you, but please don't cry. Please find it in your heart to forgive me.'

'There is nothing to forgive.'

'Oh, but there is. But I will make it up to you, I promise, if you will give me the chance. If you just—' His words were suddenly stolen by the most remarkable thing—a flutter against his cheek where it was pressed to Emma's belly. Their baby! Leo scrambled to his feet, his hand to his face as if he could somehow keep hold of the feeling.

'The baby! I felt it move!' He stared at Emma in wide-eyed astonishment, and she smiled at him. The most beautiful smile. Taking his hand, she pressed it back down on her belly.

'I know. It's amazing, isn't it? And before long he will be with us. A new life. A new start. That's what I want, Leo. Not forgiveness. No looking back. Just forward towards the future.'

'My darling Emma.' He brushed his hand against her cheek. 'When did you get to be so wise?'

'Well, one of us has to be.' The twinkle in her eyes warmed his heart, dried the last of her tears.

'*È vero.*' He smiled back, brushing her hair away from her face. He wasn't going to argue with her. 'And I promise to be the best man I can possibly be.'

'You already are that man, my love.'

'And the best father.'

'I have no doubt of that.'

'I love you, Emma Ravenino.'

'And I love you too, Leonardo. More than I can say.'

'Emma?'

'Mmm…?'

'Stop staring at me.'

Emma shifted the position of her elbow. She had been gazing at Leo ever since he'd closed his eyes, studying the beautiful face she loved so much while she had the chance. Thick dark lashes fringed his closed lids. Two fine grooves between his brows indicated his tendency to scowl with scrutiny or impatience. Straight nose, perfectly drawn mouth, jawline covered in a dark shadow of stubble. She could still feel the burn of that stubble against her face. Against her breasts, against her inner thighs…

'You are still doing it.' His eyes flickered beneath lids that were still firmly closed.

'So what if I am?' Emma teased. 'You can't stop me.'

'Hmm... Is that a challenge?' The eyelids slowly opened. 'Because you know I can't resist one of those.'

'So what are you going to do about it?'

'Let me think.' The lids half closed again. 'Ah, yes, this...'

With a rush of movement she was in his arms, her breasts crushed against his naked chest, her lips crushed beneath his.

When the need for air eventually forced them apart, Emma gazed at him again with laughing eyes. 'Okay, you won that, but only because you played dirty.'

'Not half as dirty as I'd like to be.' Leo's leg slid between her thighs, his head moving to nuzzle her neck and shoulder, pushing aside her hair until his lips found bare skin.

'Stop that, you.' Reluctantly Emma shoved him away. 'We really should get up, you know.'

'I don't see why. We can do whatever we want.' Leo moved a strand of hair away from her face. 'And right now I want to be in bed with my wife.'

'But we have been here for hours. People will be wondering where we are.'

'Who cares?'

'Cordelia maybe?' Emma swept her fringe out of her eyes.

'Cordelia is too preoccupied with Taddeo to be worrying about anything else.'

'I've met her, you know. Cordelia,' Emma admitted softly.

'You have? When?'

'After I left you in the library. I started to feel a bit faint and she helped me into the salon.'

'*Cristo*, Emma. Why didn't you say? Why didn't she come and tell me?'

'Because I asked her not to. Begged her, in fact. I couldn't face seeing you again. Not after…'

'I'm so sorry, Emma.' Leo cupped her face in his hands. 'So sorry for all the hurt and pain I have caused you. For saying that hateful thing about your mother and her boyfriend…it was unforgivable.'

'It doesn't matter.'

'Yes, it does.' He dropped his hands, raking them through his hair, his anguish clear. 'It matters that you were brave enough to open up to me about something so painful in your life and I threw it back in your face in a moment of selfish anger. It was despicable of me.'

'Then I forgive you.' Emma gazed at the storm in his eyes, instinctively wanting to take the suffering away.

'I will support you in any way I can—you do know that? Do anything within my power to make amends. I'll even try and get on with your mother, if that's what you want.' His lips twisted with a wry smile. 'We could stick her on a desert island. Buy her a commune, whatever you think best.'

'Hmm, I don't think that would work. I'm not sure you have fully grasped the principles she lives by.'

'Nor will I, until she loves you the way you deserve to be loved.'

Emma's throat tightened. She reached for Leo's hand, linking her fingers in his to bring it down on the covers between them. 'Let's just take it a day at a time and see what happens. Miracles don't happen overnight.'

'Some do.' Leo moved their hands to her stomach, his eyes shining with love.

'Yes.' Emma gazed back at him. 'They do, don't they?'

Pushing himself up against the pillows, Leo folded his arms across his chest. Bronzed skin, sculpted muscles, hard, dark nipples.

So beautiful. 'If you let me, I would like to try and give you some sort of explanation for my behaviour.'

'No…really…it's not necessary.'

'Please, Emma, let me say this.'

'Okay.' She snuggled beside him. 'If that's what you want.' But her teasing tone was met with a firming of the jaw, a swallow of the throat she could hear as well as see.

'This is not an excuse, nowhere near, but the reason I was so intent on pushing you away was because I was convinced I could never be the man you wanted me to be. That I could never give you the happy ever after you deserved.' The seriousness in his eyes broke her heart. 'I thought I had to protect you.'

'From what? I don't understand.'

'From me. From the man I was sure I was. Deep down. I thought that if I were to let you love me, if I allowed you into my heart you would see it for what it was.'

'Which is?'

'Something small and shrivelled and black.' His mouth twisted with distaste.

'No! Why ever would you think such a thing?' Shock shadowed Emma's gaze as she reached for his hand again, clasping it to her breast.

'Because that's what it felt like. I was so

consumed with bitterness and hatred over losing Ravenino I was convinced it had become all I was. I took my mother's betrayal and used it as a weapon, a protector, resolving to never let a woman close to me again. Then you came along and everything I thought I knew was thrown into doubt. You shook the very foundations of my ordered life.' He gave a soft laugh.

'And to make matters worse, I found out you had issues with your own mother. But instead of railing against her, you were still trying to build a relationship with her. I couldn't understand why you would do that, why you would carry on letting her hurt you. Now I know it's because you are a much better person than me.'

'Not better, Leo, just different.' Emma clutched his hand tightly to ward off tears, testing a watery smile. 'Okay, maybe better.'

But Leo's return smile only drew his features tighter. 'You unwittingly showed how I had let my own mother's mistake dominate my life. But I was still too stubborn to acknowledge that I was wrong, and you were right. That forgiveness is so much better than bitterness. That the dead weight I was carrying around inside me was of my own making.

'So what did I do? I fought against you as

hard as I could, distanced myself, tried to convince myself you meant nothing to me. For your sake as well as mine. But it was useless. No matter what I did, you were still there in my head, smashing through my defences, driving me crazy.'

'Oh, Leo.' Emma kissed the hand she held in hers, then moved her lips to his face, laying the softest of kisses against his mouth. But Leo edged away, determined to meet her eyes.

'When you turned up today, out of the blue, I went into a kind of shock. And that was before you told me you loved me. It was like I couldn't process the enormity of my feelings for you.

'So I walked the streets in search of vindication, fully expecting the sense of loss to kick in, for the hostility and resentment I had nurtured for so long to take over. To validate the way I had treated you. But nothing happened. All I could think of was how I had hurt you. So I had to try harder.

'I went to the graveyard, sure that the graves of my mother and Alberto would trigger the old bitterness and anger. But still there was nothing. That's when I realised the ache in my gut had nothing to do with Ravenino any more, and everything to do with you. I was about to go chasing after you when you found me. I can't tell you how it felt to see you standing there. To know you hadn't given up on me.'

'We have Cordelia to thank for that. She told me I had won your heart. I didn't believe her, but it at least gave me the courage to stay and ask you one last time.'

'Then I owe her a great debt.'

'We both do.'

'But nothing compared to the debt I owe to you, *cara*. For being strong enough to smash through the walls of my stubbornness and fear and allow me to finally see the truth.'

Emma took a breath, ready to make a confession of her own. 'You know I always thought you were still in love with Cordelia?'

'Whatever made you think that?' Leo's brow furrowed in surprise.

'I decided you could never love me because your heart still belonged to her.'

'Tesoro mio.' Leo touched her cheek with his free hand. 'I agreed to marry Cordelia out of duty, then made the mistake of thinking I should honour the agreement, even when I lost the principality. My pride was hurt, I'll admit, but I never loved her.'

For a moment they just stared into one another's eyes, the spilling of confessions laying them bare.

'You know I would never have accepted that description of your heart, even if you couldn't love me.' Emma's solemn words broke the silence. 'I have seen your kindness and generosity time and again, even when you have tried to hide them from me. The way you have helped Beatrice and her family. The respect you show your staff, the employees of your companies. The charities you support.'

'Supporting people financially is easy.' The backs of his fingers smoothed over her chin, down her neck. 'My mistake was thinking I could do that with you. That that would be enough. And when I found it wasn't, that I wanted all of you, not just your company, your body, your lovely face across the table from me at breakfast, but your heart and your soul as well—then I knew I was in deep trouble.'

'Darling Leo.' Emma gazed at him. 'You have all of those things. Plus my undying love. Now and for ever.'

'Then I have so much more than I deserve.'

'I love you, Leo, so very much.'

'And I love you. So much more.'

Enveloping her in his arms, Leo lowered his head, finding her lips to deliver the sweetest, most tender kiss in the world.

EPILOGUE

'Do you think we should go and rescue them from our son?' Behind him, Leo could hear Emma moving around the room, collecting up their belongings.

He looked out of the bedroom window to where the small group had settled themselves under the shade of an ancient oak tree. A rug had been laid out, the remains of an impromptu picnic scattered around them, and baby Carlo was being tossed in the air by his doting uncle. Even though Leo couldn't hear it, he knew his son would be chuckling uncontrollably. Leo loved that chuckle. It was the most joyous sound in the world.

Joining him, Emma rested her chin on his shoulder, sliding her arms around his waist.

'No, let's leave them to it.' Leo squeezed her hands. 'They look like they are having fun. Besides, it's good practice for Taddeo.'

'No! What…? You mean…?'

'*Sì, cara*, it's true.' He turned to smile at his wife. 'Taddeo told me this morning. Cordelia is pregnant.'

'How wonderful!' Emma's face lit up. 'A little cousin for Carlo! I'm so pleased!'

They both watched as Carlo was passed to Cordelia, who confidently straightened his little sun hat, redid the ties, then kissed him on the nose.

'So we could have the next Conte di Ravenino in the making?' She posed the question lightly, but Leo could sense the tinge of anxiety.

'We could indeed. And there's no need to look like that, *amore mio*. I have fully accepted that Taddeo is the rightful Conte, and his son will carry on the line.'

'No regrets?' Her gaze searched his face.

'None whatever. How could I when I have you and Carlo? You are so much more precious than any piece of land or title.'

Emma smiled, touching her finger to his lips. They had been living at the Castello on and off for almost nine months now. Carlo had been born here. But they both knew their stay was only temporary. And despite Leo's reassurances, a little bit of Emma still worried that he would find it hard to leave.

'Do you think Taddeo will cope on his own? Without you to support him?'

Leo shrugged. 'I'll still be available if he needs me, but it's time he stood on his own two feet. And you know what, I think he'll be fine. The accident was the best thing that could have happened to him.'

'Leo!'

'I mean it. It seems to have finally knocked some sense into him.'

'I'm not sure he'd see it like that. But he told me himself that he feels much more confident now. Ready to rule.'

'About time. But if he dares to use that phrase on social media, I will kill him.'

'Don't be such a grouch.' Emma laughed. 'He's very grateful, you know, for everything you've done while he's been recovering.'

'I know. But it's time to hand over the reins now. We have our own lives to get on with. And to be honest, I can't wait.'

'Me too.' Emma gazed up at his handsome face. Grey eyes stared back at her, clear and bright. Shining, not with doubt or regret but with love. It was time to stop worrying.

'Speaking of which, what time are we flying back to Milan?' She crossed back into the room, where an array of Carlo's adorable baby clothes were spread on the bed. 'I need to get on with this packing.'

'Staff are employed for that job.' Leo walked behind her. 'I need my wife for far more important activities.'

'Such as?'

'Well, if Carlo is being entertained elsewhere it seems a shame to waste the opportunity.'

'Leonardo Ravenino, you are incorrigible.' Her stern voice didn't fool either of them. 'I'm sure you must have matters of state to discuss with Taddeo before we leave.'

'The state can wait.'

'Another quote for social media?'

'Ha!' Laughing, Leo smothered her in his arms, pressing the length of his body against hers. So tall and strong, taut muscles beneath warm flesh. Closing her eyes, Emma moulded herself against him.

'Oh, I nearly forgot.' Leo loosened his hold. 'I saw something in the press this morning that will interest you.' He moved into the bedroom, searching around. 'Where did I put it? Ah, here it is.'

He held up a newspaper in his hands and the two of them exchanged a glance. It was a copy of the *Paladin*.

'Not another reporter getting into terrible trouble by submitting the wrong article?' Emma came to stand beside him.

'No, not this time. Although that didn't turn out so badly in the end, did it?' Leo turned to face her, love shining in his eyes.

Sitting them on the edge of the bed, he turned over the pages until he found what he was looking for, a report on a recent G7 conference on homelessness. 'Here, listen to this: *"World leaders agreed that much more needed to be done, both nationally and internationally. The charitable foundation Read All About It was cited as an excellent example of an innovative approach to raising both awareness and funding."'*

'Ooh, that's great publicity for us.' Emma took the newspaper from his hands to read it for herself. 'I'll make sure the team know about this.'

'Never mind the publicity.' Leo stopped the hand that was reaching for her phone. 'How about taking a minute to give yourself some praise? What you have achieved is incredible. I am so proud of you.'

'Thank you.' Emma reached to touch his lips with her own. 'I'm proud of myself too. Though technically it was your idea.'

'But you made it happen.'

'Yes, I did, didn't I?' She rested her head on his shoulder.

'And you don't regret not working for the *Paladin* any more?'

'No, of course not!' Emma sat upright, turning to take Leo's face in her hands. The face she loved so much. The newspaper slid to the floor. 'How could I possibly regret anything now that I have you and Carlo? My life has never been more perfect. It never could be.'

It was true. Finally Emma felt like she belonged. Not the lost child trying to fit in with her chaotic family in the wilds of the countryside. Not in London, struggling to make ends meet, or trying to prove herself at the offices of the *Paladin*. But with Leo, as a wife and a mother. And not only that but she had a career she loved too and the full support of a husband to make it happen. No longer Emma Quinn but Emma Ravenino, she finally knew who she was.

'I'm so glad.' Leo removed her hands, kissing her knuckles. 'I would hate to think I might have to start trying to make it up to you again. You know where that leads.'

'Mmm…yes, I do.' Emma felt herself being lifted up onto the bed, gently laid back across the pillows. 'It's a penance I have to bear.'

'And can I say you do it with great fortitude.' Leo lay down beside her, putting his arms around her again, drawing her to him, lightly kissing her forehead, her cheeks, her lips.

'Thank you. I do my best.'

'*Ti amo, mia bella* Emma.'

'And I love you too, Leo. Always and for ever.'

Emma had just enough time to say the words before Leo's mouth was on hers again. For a moment they both caught the light in each other's eyes before the power of the kiss took over, and their lids closed in surrendered bliss.

* * * * *

Captivated by From Exposé to Expecting?
*You won't be able to resist
these other stories
by Andie Brock!*

Bound by His Desert Diamond
The Greek's Pleasurable Revenge
Vieri's Convenient Vows
Kidnapped for Her Secret Son
Reunited by the Greek's Vows

Available now!